Praise for *Whispered Memories*

'*Whispered Memories* is a fascin.
hope and the intriguing possib.
life. It draws you in emotionally
guessing right until the end.'
Suzy Parsons, author of *Unsuitable*

'Inspired ... It's a must read ... I didn't put this book down at all, the storyline has all it requires to reel you into the worlds of the characters ... This is clever, brilliant, inspired writing and I hope we see a lot more of this author.'
Amazon reader

'Have just finished this amazing story. Well done, Nicola. You kept me up well into the early hours.'
Amazon reader

'Brilliant book ... There is a great cast of characters, with plots and twists. Looking forward to the next book by this author.'
Amazon reader

'Gripping and compelling. Nicola knows how to connect you to the characters. I think I'll start again now I've finished.'
Amazon reader

'What a rollercoaster of emotion. The book is so full of love that it almost jumps out of the page. For a first book it is amazing. I can't wait to read the next.'
Amazon reader

Within the
Silence

Also by Nicola Avery:

Whispered Memories

To Peter
Thank you
Nicola xx

Within the Silence

Nicola Avery . *com*

ISBN: 978-1-911195-78-8

Also available as an ebook
ISBN: 978-1-911195-79-5

Typeset by Jill Sawyer
Cover design by Berni Stevens
Author photograph © Nicola Light Photography

Printed and bound in Great Britain by Clays Ltd, Elcograf S.p.A.

For Charlie, Melinda and Harriet – Always

Matt. 18:16 'But who so shall offend one of these little ones … it were better for him that a milestone were hanged about his neck and that he were drowned in the depth of the sea.'

Prologue

The windscreen wipers beat as frantically as Tilly Stone's heart as she threw the Volkswagen Golf's steering wheel over to the right and screeched onto the rain-drenched tarmac of the main road. The wet rubber tyres squealed in unison with the cries from her four-year-old daughter, Maddy, strapped tightly into her car seat in the back of the speeding vehicle.

Tilly's eyes left the road momentarily to meet those of her daughter, hauntingly reflected in the rear-view mirror. Dressed in her pale blue pyjamas, her blonde hair statically spiked across the fabric of her seat, tiny Madeline Stone looked back at her mother imploringly.

'Mummy's got you, darling. It's going to be all right now,' said Tilly, with a forced faint smile, her stomach knotting with the sickening realisation of what she'd just discovered.

At that exact moment, further down the same road, a dog ran out in front of an oncoming car, forcing it to change lanes. The sound of a car horn alerted Tilly to the headlights looming closer on the wrong side of the road. Reacting to the onrushing danger, she steered the Volkswagen away from the lights, losing control on the slippery road and sending the car spinning.

For Tilly, the next few seconds played out slowly as she helplessly watched the approaching street lamp and wall. The impact of metal on concrete killed her outright. She never had time to tell her daughter she loved her.

Tilly's husband, Jon Stone, was distraught. The fact that the accident occurred so close to their home somehow made it all the more distressing. Sympathy for his loss came in abundance. As a pillar of local society, and a revered consultant psychiatrist specialising in child and adolescent psychiatry, Jon Stone stoically resumed his life and took full responsibility for bringing up his only child, Maddy.

Not one person questioned where Tilly had been going at that time of night, with her daughter – and in such a hurry.

Chapter 1

M addy Stone stood beside the wall that offered protection to the manicured native garden looking out across the flat Mediterranean Sea. Below her, a trail of steep steps roughly hewn into the hard rock and framed in part by tall Balearic island plants wound down to the old fisherman's jetty and the tiny strip of beach. This secluded Majorcan inlet, accessible only by water or determined hikers, accommodated a few small dinghies tonight.

Maddy's father, Jon Stone, was hosting an engagement party for her stepsister Zara, to which a number of locals and neighbouring summertime visitors had been invited. In the distance, she could hear the music playing – blues and jazz, Zara's favourite. But Maddy's heart ached for the sounds of the sea back down on the jetty, the slapping of the water against the helm of her boat or the dull squeak of the dinghies rubbing against one another.

She remained perfectly still, enjoying the view. Above her, a lone gull swooped low across the bay calling out for its mate, as she watched a blood-orange sun finally slipping below the horizon, swallowed again for today by a stretch of endless grey-glass sea. Wrapping her arms around her slim body, Maddy shivered, hastily brushing away the solitary tear that slipped silently down her face. The soft evening breeze caught on a tendril of her blonde hair, and she carelessly twisted and tucked it behind her ear, momentarily forgetting her precious diamond studs: an heirloom from her grandmother's estate and given to her on her twenty-first birthday.

She could hear the closing murmurs from the evening's celebrations now, trickling out through the villa's open doors. She stood between two such different worlds – both of them hers and both about to collide.

Throughout her life, Maddy had kept her secrets safe: *from* the ones she loved and *for* the ones she loved. Only now, it was almost time to stop pretending, forever. She knew she must be patient for just a little while longer. What she was about to do would hurt those she loved the most, and she wanted Zara to enjoy her special evening. Tomorrow, she'd take back control of her own life, whatever the consequences.

On a thin gold chain around her neck hung a gold filigree ring, one of a pair of two entwined dolphins. An inexpensive trinket bought in the Old Town of Ibiza. Rubbing the ring between her fingers, Maddy raised it to her lips, her mouth gently kissing the warm metal. Breathing in slowly and deeply, she willed her racing heart to calm. It would be time soon enough; the party was winding up.

Unaware that she was being watched, Maddy turned away from the sea, tucking the necklace and ring safely between her breasts. She walked back towards the lights of the villa. Time to play the perfect daughter, the loving sister. After tomorrow, nothing would ever be the same again, for any of them.

Nervous but resolved, Maddy had begun to explain her intentions in a note for Zara, slipping it into her bedside drawer to complete later. She smiled now, with mixed emotions, glancing one more time at the hauntingly beautiful beach-cove scene on her bedroom wall. Taking a final look behind her, she quietly slipped out to the garden through the connecting door, closing the door gently.

They'd arranged to meet after the party, on the jetty, after everyone had retired for the night. The guests were long gone now and the villa slept soundlessly. Torch in hand, Maddy crossed the coarse goose grass, avoiding the sprinklers, on towards the steep footpath leading down to the beach. The strategically placed lights on the sloping garden bank highlighted enough of the treacherous undulating levels and the crudely formed steps. As she neared the bottom of the pathway, she recognised the familiar smell of his aftershave, now mingling with that of the pines and sea. Her heart missed a beat. There was no going back.

Chapter 2

*Z*ara Hopper lay awake. The excitement of last night's festivities still buzzed around her head. *What a party!* Carefully twisting her body, she silently slipped out of bed and into the en-suite bathroom. The stone floor felt pleasantly cool to her bare feet as she filled her toothbrush mug with water from the tap. Swallowing most of the contents, she paused, frowning. *Oh, God*, she thought. *What's the rule about the tap water here? Can I drink it or not?* Placing the mug to one side, she smiled at her reflection. At twenty-five, Zara was well aware that the combination of excessive alcohol and no sleep took its toll, but she had to laugh at the face that stared back at her. Her mid-length, dark hair, curly and thick on its best days, bounced out of control around her pretty, round face, and her warm brown eyes were outlined by black smudges as a result of hastily removed mascara. 'Ugh!' she whispered. 'God, you look awful!'

Sticking out her tongue, she groaned at its appearance in the mirror – flat and pale pink with creamy fur. Sucking in her cheeks, she tried to curl her tongue up on either side and failed again. This was a trick that Maddy and their adoptive sister, Pippa, had learnt, showing off their skills at tongue 'sausaging' whenever competition necessitated. They always won. Zara couldn't even make it to first base, no matter how hard she practised. She had never fully understood why Pippa seemed a natural, and had mastered the art before her. 'Revolting!' she mumbled to herself, scraping her tongue on a wet flannel and tossing it into the bath. One more glance at her tanned face and she smiled before returning to the bedroom.

Gareth lay on his back snoring, his mouth open. One long, muscular leg hung heavily off the bed, pulling down part of the covers and exposing his tanned torso and flat stomach. A fan of honey-coloured hair from his long fringe lay across his sunburnt nose, and Zara watched his snoring in fascination, the way his sleep-drenched breath blew up or drew down those trembling hairs.

So this is the man I'm going to marry! she thought, grinning to herself as she remembered her own reflection in the bath-room mirror. *Ah, well-matched I'd say*, and she proceeded to push open the connecting door onto the garden.

It was still early and the villa's grounds were silent except for the cries of the resident gulls and the gurgling pool filter. Not even Emily, the housekeeper, and her husband, Pedro, the gardener and handyman, were around, having been given the day off. Reclaiming her damp swimsuit from behind the pool's shower cubicle, Zara changed, discarding her oversized striped nightshirt for body-hugging Lycra. There was a mild scent of pine and rosemary wafting across the patio, where big glazed terracotta pots, overfilled with Majorcan plants and herbs, were carefully positioned along the back wall. Under a sail-shaped canopy stood a large glass and chrome table. Eight rattan armchairs with blue-and-white striped cushions were tucked alongside. The party had been kept away from the poolside, for obvious reasons, and the silent army of hired help had replaced most of the garden furniture at the time of the final guests leaving. Jon Stone always knew how to hold a successful func-tion, his famous mantra: 'The secret of enjoyment for everyone is to ensure there is no mess at the end!'

Entering the pool, Zara noted the abandoned towel hanging over the back of one of the chairs. *Ah … perhaps Maddy's up, after all,* she thought as she started her lengths.

Zara's mother, Lisa Hopper, had married Jon when Zara was nineteen. Widowed in her thirties, when Zara was just ten, she had never imagined looking for a replacement husband. That was until she met Jon. For Zara, his introduction into their lives meant she could happily relinquish the weighty responsibility for her mother's happiness.

There were many changes in her life as a result of her mother's marriage. Among these were the introduction of a sixteen-year-old stepsister called Maddy and the adoption of a little girl called Pippa. Zara had gone from being an only child to being one of three girls in the space of a year, and loved it.

Jon's daughter, Maddy, was an enigma: a tall and willowy blonde with an enviable bone structure and flashing sea-green eyes that missed nothing, framed by dark brows and dark lashes. Maddy had never dressed provocatively, even in her teens, preferring to drape her slim, athletic frame in loose and shapeless clothing, and wearing her blonde hair cut and feathered just below her chin. Despite this seemingly deliberate attempt to lessen her feminine appeal, Maddy's natural beauty and raw sexuality always shone through, much to Zara's good-natured irritation.

At the time of Jon's romancing of Zara's mother, Maddy had been away in Majorca, learning Spanish, cookery and how to sail. Zara had been envious of the life that had been chosen for her stepsister. She didn't meet her until the month before her mother's wedding and had, in her mind, created an image of a spoilt and affected only child. When they finally met, Zara had been surprised by her quiet, gentle and unassuming manner. As an only child herself, she recognised the guarded loneliness and reached out to Maddy.

For her part, Maddy, having become motherless at an early age, had grown up quickly, abandoning her childhood sooner than most. Although younger than Zara, she displayed a maturity beyond her years. Starved of sibling companionship, Maddy warily accepted Zara's unconditional friendship and a bond developed between the two girls. In time, each would do anything for the other.

Prior to her wedding, Zara's mother, an attractive, older version of her daughter, had announced to a surprised family and close friends her intention to try for another baby. But after the disappointing news that Jon's vasectomy reversal had proved unsuccessful, Lisa reluctantly accepted that Nature had won.

It was Jon's friend, Doctor Nathan Collins, who provided the newlyweds with the perfect solution: the private adoption of a child 'known' to him. It had all happened so fast and so seamlessly for an ecstatic Lisa; Jon and Nathan saw to all the legalities surrounding the adoption, and little Pippa Stone joined her newly created family aged eight months. Lisa fell in love with her newest daughter, instantly. Pippa's trusting manner and quick smile captivated hearts from the moment she arrived. There was never a need for babysitters or home help when Zara and Maddy were around. Both girls happily lavished their attention on their new sister, bathing, dressing, feeding and entertaining her. It seemed Pippa was never to be found without at least one female member of the household hovering about her. Maddy had even been known to tuck herself up in Pippa's bed on nights when Lisa was ill, overtired or stayed out late, and she worked through her diary with Zara to ensure Lisa always had cover. For Lisa, an older mother and newly married, the help from the girls proved invaluable and she never missed an opportunity to advise Jon of this.

Generous to a fault, Lisa also never suggested that either grown daughter should find her own place to live. The house in Wimbledon had enough space for everyone, even for Gareth on the nights he stayed over.

As for little Pippa, she felt wanted and loved from the very moment she entered the household. For her new father, Jon, Pippa became the perfect addition to his family. For Zara, she was the little sister she never had. And for Maddy? Well, Maddy thought Pippa 'a gift from God'.

Dripping wet, Zara padded across the manicured lawn towards the garden wall. The grass felt coarse and springy beneath her feet and she wished she had put some shoes on. From here she could see out to sea and part of the old fisherman's jetty where Maddy's sailing boat bobbed quietly in the sheltered waters.

An experienced sailor, Maddy had bought her Beneteau boat with some of the money from her deceased mother's estate. With her offshore instructor certifications, Maddy's dream of a life as a sailing instructor on the Balearic Islands was all but realised. She'd taken possession of her new boat in Palma, Majorca, naming it the *Phoenix*, and when staying in her grandmother's old Pink Villa, would moor inside the deep sheltered waters of the *cala*. The local fishermen and the owners of the few holiday homes within this inlet knew Maddy and the *Phoenix* by sight, and turned a blind eye to her mooring on the deep jetty. For Maddy, the purchase of the *Phoenix* represented a new start – hence the name – giving her the freedom to sail wherever and whenever she wanted. This summer, content with the Majorcan bays, she'd dropped the hook and stayed out for days, returning relaxed and tanned, to restock the boat or spend precious time with Pippa, teaching her the basics of seamanship. It was here, on the waters in Majorca, living in the Pink Villa, that Maddy was happiest, like her grandmother before her. Sailing in the warm waters around Majorca and Ibiza allowed her to reflect on her life, making plans for the future. She claimed these waters had the ability to rejuvenate her very soul, repairing the unfairness of the past and bringing her safely to the moment. And so, emotionally cleansed, she would share her love of the sea with Zara and Pippa, taking them to the tiny unreachable and secret beaches, where they'd swim contentedly under the sail and sun. She never took her father out on the *Phoenix* and he never asked to go with her; he and Lisa preferred his boat – no sails, a large engine and a carpeted saloon with a well-stocked bar.

Zara could just make out the *Phoenix* alongside the jetty, but there was no sign of Maddy, even on the visible parts of the pathway down to the beach. She waited and watched for a moment, but still no one approached from the main house or up from the beach. Shrugging her shoulders, Zara made her way back to the villa.

Pippa Stone was just six years old and already the darling of the locals in Majorca – perfectly formed, although still tiny for her age, with long blonde, wavy hair, large brown eyes and skin that turned golden brown under the sun.

Pippa carefully untangled herself from the cream bedsheets and wandered out of her bedroom. Knowing the rule about swimming unaccompanied, she padded the villa floor, looking for one of her sisters. She opened Maddy's door first. Normally in the mornings, she would crawl into bed with her sister, curling up for a sleepy hug, but this morning the bed was already made up. With no concept of time, Pippa then walked towards her parents' room and, pushing open the door, she crept up to her father's bedside.

'Hello, Daddy,' she whispered.

Jon opened one eye and, seeing Pippa, he grinned. 'Hello, beautiful. Do you want to come in with Daddy?'

'No, I'm looking for Maddy.' Nevertheless, Pippa felt herself being lifted and tucked into her father's arms. 'Not so tight!' she cried, struggling against the intensity and heat of her father's embrace. 'I don't like it so tight,' she whined, squirming in his hold.

'Jon,' said Lisa firmly. 'Leave her. You're too forceful with her.'

There was a pause as Pippa extricated herself.

'Do you want to come over to my side?' Lisa asked, lifting the covers slightly.

'Yes,' Pippa answered, and Jon reluctantly let her scramble over his legs to reach Lisa's side, her pyjama-clad bottom raised in her escape.

'Are you hungry, sweetheart? Shall we get Daddy to make you some breakfast?' Lisa asked as Pippa threw her arms lovingly around her neck.

'No, I'll wait for Maddy. I like her breakfasts best!'

Lisa smiled, pushing back her daughter's hair from her face. 'You love your Maddy, don't you?'

Pippa nodded, burying her head in her mother's warm body under the covers before answering in a muffled voice, 'And I love you!'

Lisa looked over at her husband's reclining form. 'What time did you get to bed last night? I woke at about four thirty and you weren't here.'

Lying back on his side of the bed, Jon paused before replying. 'Not sure. I had some business to take care of with Nathan. Thought I was back earlier than that – I could have been in the bathroom?'

Pippa emerged from her warm hiding place, climbing out of the covers and stepping onto the cream stone floor.

'Can I find the girls, Mummy?'

'Good idea', Lisa said. 'Then perhaps we could all have breakfast. What's the time?'

'Seven forty-five!' groaned Jon, swinging his bare legs out of bed.

Lisa watched her husband's tanned and naked body move towards the bathroom. 'Jon!' she cried as Pippa shrieked, diving back into the bed and under the covers, laughing uncontrollably. 'I do wish you'd put something on, Jon. It's not a pretty sight for poor Pippa, not at your age. It's not nice, is it Pippa?'

Gasping for breath, Pippa laughed. 'No. It's horrid,' she said and snuggled back into her mother's warm body.

'Jon?' Lisa called out, lifting her head from her daughter's embrace. 'Did you hear me?' There was the sound of someone peeing, then the flushing of the toilet.

'And *please* shut the door,' wailed Lisa as she tickled a giggling and breathless Pippa. 'He's such a naughty Daddy, isn't he?'

Covering her eyes, Pippa waited until Jon's naked form climbed back into bed, then she dropped back onto the bedroom floor and ran out along the corridor, bursting out onto the garden terrace as Zara walked towards her, towel-clad and smiling.

'You've been swimming already!' Pippa scolded.

'Less of the attitude, missy,' said Zara, unwrapping her towel just enough to envelop her wriggling, laughing sister.

'Can we go swimming now?' Pippa asked, her smiling face lifted towards her sister's.

'You can come in with me in a minute,' answered Zara, acknowledging Jon's presence on the pool terrace.

'Morning, Zara,' Jon said, moving towards her and kissing her on the cheek. 'Did you sleep well? And where's Gareth?'

Zara smiled. 'Last time I looked he was flat on his back, catching flies and snoring loudly.'

'Some of us don't have such luck, do we?' said Jon, pointedly looking at Pippa, who bounced off across the grass towards the pathway leading down to the beach.

'Have you seen Maddy?' called Pippa, looking out at the *Phoenix*.

'No, I haven't seen her yet,' replied Zara, watching Pippa's shoulders drop in disappointment. 'Are you sure she's not still asleep?'

'Nope,' said Pippa, returning to the patio. 'Her bed's made up, so she must be down on the beach or on her boat. Can I go down and get her? We're going out to the secret beach today, and she'll need a good breakfast. And I want to check if my stuff's already on board.'

Zara laughed as she attempted to hold onto her excited sister. 'Wait a moment, sweetie, you can't go down in your PJs.'

'Oh!' Pippa exclaimed, laughing as she peeled off her favourite *Frozen* pyjamas and tossed them under the table before running to get her tiny red swimsuit which was hanging by the showers. 'I forgot. Nearly ready,' she shouted, wriggling into the tight costume.

'Here, let me help you,' Jon offered, moving towards her.

'No thank you, Daddy. I can do it myself,' she answered.

Zara smiled at her sister's feisty independence – and the fact that her bathing costume straps were all twisted around one armpit. Quickly re-adjusting the tiny costume, Zara grinned. 'Why don't we leave Maddy for a bit? She could be sleeping on the beach; you know how she loves the early mornings down there. She'll come up when she's ready.'

'But it's late. We've got lots to do today. She told me. And I need to make sure she hasn't forgotten our plans.'

Zara dropped to one knee, pulling Pippa towards her and kissing her on the nose. 'It's still early, especially after a party. I'm sure she hasn't forgotten.'

Pippa moved away from Zara, standing perfectly still as she stared longingly out to sea. Then, turning back towards her sister, she tried again. '*Please* come with me, Zara. I can't go down there on my own. You know Daddy's rules ...' Pippa tilted her head in her father's direction, then gave Zara one of her lopsided grins.

Zara laughed. 'Ok, you win! Let me find some shoes and I'll take you down.'

'Thought we were going to have breakfast?' asked Jon, returning to the table with his laptop.

'We will. I'll just take Pippa down to the jetty and collect Maddy, if she's down there. We won't be long, I promise,' she said, looking around for some footwear. 'Now, shoes ... where did I leave them?'

'There!' Pippa pointed and ran onto the grass, returning with a pair of well-worn flip-flops. Flinging them over to Zara, she crammed her little tanned toes into her own bright pink jellies.

Zara laughed at Pippa's eager face, then threw an oversized T-shirt over her damp swimsuit, running her hands quickly through her waterlogged curls. 'Back soon,' she told Jon, who had made himself comfortable at the table. 'Tell Gareth, if he's up, where I've gone,' she added, before running to catch up as Pippa started the descent to the beach. 'Careful, Pippa. Remember, I don't like this uneven bit. Please keep to the garden side ... and slow down, you're making me nervous.'

The rocky pathway, steep and winding in parts, had been responsible for a number of Pippa's holiday tumbles. On the garden side stood a high bank planted with shrubs and trees, some native Majorcan, others imported, but all carefully chosen for privacy purposes. On the other side was just a steep drop onto the pink-coloured rocks below. This route up from the beach did little to encourage trespassers into the gardens.

'Don't worry,' Pippa's sing-song voice replied as she deliberately tucked herself closer to the bank, her little legs and feet braced to accommodate the uneven causeway. 'I'm being careful.'

Zara quickened her pace to catch up.

Jon watched the girls as they made their way down the pathway, up to the point where the tall trees and foliage hid them from view. Then, turning, he smiled to himself and made his way back to the table, now being laid for breakfast by Lisa, her dark damp hair swept up into a nest of curls. She kissed him quickly on the mouth as he patted her curvaceous bottom through her swimming costume.

'Girls?' she asked, folding a napkin and tossing it onto a white side plate.

'Collecting Maddy for breakfast.'

'Gareth?'

'Sleeping.'

'And Nathan?'

'Haven't seen him yet. Must still be in the guest house.'

'Should we call him for breakfast?' Lisa asked.

'No, he looked exhausted last night. Let's leave him. He'll join us later when he's ready.'

'Orange juice?' Lisa asked, a jug poised over Jon's glass. As she began to pour, a piercing scream cut through the air. 'That's Pippa!' she cried. Dropping the glass jug, she kicked back her chair and ran in the direction of the scream.

Slower to react, Jon had time to observe the glass jug drop, shattering on contact with the table, the broken glass, together

14

with slices of blood oranges, now lying in a haphazard pile. He experienced a momentary flash of disquiet before running towards the beach descent, shouting for Nathan and Gareth as he did so.

Chapter 3

Pippa stood at the edge of the pathway, staring down at a figure on the rocks below her. 'Maddy,' she whimpered, looking first at Zara for confirmation, then back down to where the body lay. Zara held her breath as the image came into view. Standing next to Pippa, she followed her gaze.

Maddy lay broken over the sun-bleached rocks, like a marionette, still dressed in the beautiful pale yellow dress she'd worn for the engagement party the night before. Zara had chosen it. She remembered with a pang the difficulty she'd had persuading Maddy to buy it.

'It's so girly!' Maddy had protested, standing deliberately awkwardly in the diaphanous dress. 'Just not me.'

'Oh, but it's so beautiful on you, and very different to what you'd normally wear. You'll surprise everyone. Please wear it. For me.'

Maddy had turned, checking her image in the mirror. 'Makes my legs look like Bambi's and my bottom huge!'

Zara had smiled with affection. If only Maddy had known how amazing her long, tanned legs looked in the dress, and how the material floated over her perfectly formed bottom.

'The dress is to die for, Maddy. Please humour me and wear it at my engagement party.'

To die for! thought Zara now, staring down at the crumpled body on the rocks. A faint cry escaped her lips as she pulled her pale-faced sister towards her.

'Is she alive?' asked Pippa.

Zara knew that the tide didn't reach those rocks, so there

was a chance that Maddy could still be breathing, providing she'd survived the fall. Grabbing Pippa by the shoulders, she stared into her eyes. 'Pippa,' she said, 'I need you to go back now for help. Tell Mummy and Jon what's happened and tell them we need Uncle Nathan … and an ambulance.' Zara looked at Pippa's bloodless face as she nodded, mutely. 'Now hurry, sweetie. I'm going to climb down to Maddy.'

'But is she alive?' Pippa asked again, her body beginning to tremble.

Zara glanced down to the rocks below once more. In her heart she feared the worst, but looking into Pippa's eyes, brimming with tears, she told her, 'If anyone can survive a fall like that, it will be our Maddy. Now you go back to the villa and get help. I'll go down to Maddy,' she repeated.

Zara watched the small figure make her way up the path, carefully keeping to the garden side. Once Pippa was out of sight, Zara made her own way down, dropping onto the beach descent. From there, she climbed up and back across the jagged rock formation to reach Maddy. A gull dived low above her, its mournful cry echoing her own, as she jammed her hand into her mouth to stifle her next sob. 'Oh, my beautiful Maddy,' she whimpered, dropping onto her haunches and reaching for her wrist. There was a faint pulse.

'Hold on, Maddy, I'm here. It's Zara, darling. I'm here with you. Do you hear me? We're going to get you help.'

Zara carefully balanced herself on the rough rocks, her shaking hands gently stroking the bloodied hair off Maddy's face.

'Don't give up on me now,' she begged.

Maddy lay at an unnatural angle, her head and outstretched neck to one side of her twisted torso. One of her long, tanned legs, awkwardly bent, lay trapped under her splayed body. Zara held Maddy's hand in hers, gently kissing the grazed and bleeding knuckles.

'Don't go anywhere, Maddy … Stay with me … Help's on its way.'

Zara looked up to the pathway above as a group of people came into view, running. 'Here!' she shouted, letting go of Maddy's hand and waving desperately. 'Over here. Maddy's hurt!'

Sleep-tousled, unshaven and visibly shaken, Doctor Nathan Collins crouched down beside Zara as he gently examined Maddy. Lisa, trembling with shock, stood close by, clasping one of Pippa's hands.

'Alive?' asked Jon, his voice calm and controlled, despite the unravelling tragedy.

Nathan looked up at him. 'Just,' he replied, watching Jon move away from the body of his daughter.

'Can we move her?' asked Gareth, looking from Jon to Nathan.

'No,' said Nathan. 'I'd be afraid to move her without professional assistance and the right equipment. Look at the angle of her neck. Her spine could be damaged. We'll have to wait until the paramedics get here.'

'Do they understand she's fallen onto the rocks?' Zara asked. 'Will they send a helicopter?'

Jon sat stoically on one side of the rocks, his head upright, face turned away. He said nothing. Nathan glanced in his direction before replying. 'Yes, I told them. They know this region of coastland, and they couldn't use a helicopter here, Zara – too much wind and too many trees.'

Zara glanced up at the thick foliage surrounding them. *Oh, what a price for privacy*, she thought, turning back to Maddy.

'What about a boat, via the beach approach?' asked Gareth, moving closer, his eyes widening with horror at what he saw.

Nathan shook his head, sadly. 'If there's a possible neck or back injury, they won't use a boat. Too dangerous on the waves.'

'So how will they get to her?' asked Zara, her face taut with fear.

'The same way we did,' replied Nathan. 'They'll send someone down here first, to determine the extent of the injuries. Then they'll decide how best to get her up to the main lawn and into an ambulance.'

Maddy lay as she had fallen, a thin blanket fetched from the villa draped over her still form. Holding a limp wrist in his hand, Nathan looked up at the pathway above. 'But they need to hurry up,' he said. 'Her pulse is very weak ...'

Zara looked towards her mother and then Jon, desperately searching for answers. Lisa's face was drained of all colour while a sobbing Pippa buried her face in her mother's body.

'Please don't die, Maddy,' Lisa whispered, barely able to contain her emotions. Gareth moved closer to her and placed a reassuring arm around her shoulders. Zara's tears now fell unchecked as she inwardly pleaded with God for Maddy's life.

'I can only hope ...' Jon volunteered in a flat voice, leaving his sentence unfinished.

The huddled group fell into silence waiting for the paramedics. They felt a glimmer of hope as members of the Guardia Civil and two from the paramedic team came into view, descending onto their tiny beach before clambering over the rocks towards them.

'Why the Guardia Civil?' Lisa asked, alarmed.

'I suppose they have to register the accident,' suggested Gareth, looking over at Jon, who now moved towards Nathan and the paramedics and closer to Maddy's body.

Reluctantly, Zara stepped aside, allowing the rescue team greater access. She watched in desperate hope as one of the paramedics assessing the situation relayed instructions on his radio to the rest of his team. For Zara, it was the longest and most excruciating wait she'd ever experienced. Linking arms with her mother, with Pippa protectively tucked between the two of them, she silently watched as a neck brace was fitted onto Maddy.

Nathan stood, stretching his long legs, then moved quietly over to the women. 'It's ok, they've given her morphine for the pain and secured her as best they can. Now they need to move her carefully up the pathway.'

'How long will it take them to get her to hospital?' asked Lisa, gathering Pippa and Zara, both sobbing, into her arms as they all watched Maddy's body being carried away.

'Too long,' replied Nathan under his breath.

Once up on the lawn, the gathered group watched the paramedics transfer Maddy's body to the ambulance then close the doors firmly behind her. Having given preliminary details to the Guardia Civil officer, Jon and Nathan now waited for the ambulance to leave for the hospital in Palma. The whoop of a siren sounded and the vehicle finally crunched back over the gravel and pushed out onto the main road.

'We need to follow them,' said Gareth, his face ashen as he bundled Zara and Pippa into the car.

'Agreed. I'll take Jon and Lisa with me,' Nathan suggested.

'No! I want Mummy to come with me,' whined a frightened Pippa, climbing back out of Gareth's car.

Gareth looked at Nathan, who nodded in agreement. 'Fine. Lisa, you're with us,' he said.

They had all hurriedly dressed, grabbing basic clothing, footwear and their phones. Zara realised now that she had put her pale blue sundress on inside out, and her frantic fingers unconsciously pulled at the raised stitching of the hem as Gareth negotiated the difficult coastal road. Behind them, Nathan drove a dark blue Range Rover. Jon sat tight-lipped in the front passenger seat. There was no need for conversation. Jon knew that Nathan would do whatever was necessary; the two of them went back a long way, and Jon had helped Nathan in the past. Something neither had forgotten.

Chapter 4

Maddy Stone was rushed through the main accident-and-emergency doors, into an operating theatre where a crash team attempted to resuscitate her. Her damaged body shuddered as the defibrillator shocked her heart, daring her to stay. Maddy knew there were people around her, but she couldn't reach them. Try as she would, she couldn't respond. She heard their voices, but it was like wading through thick treacle and she felt so tired from the effort. The struggle to make contact with them filled her with pain, and the pull from the heavy treacle was getting stronger. Then her heart felt another punch from the paddles and the treacle shifted to one side.

'Come on, Maddy!' urged the Spanish doctor.

Another hit, then nothing. Maddy was broken – physically and emotionally. So she simply stopped fighting, allowing herself to glide away from her ruined body, floating up into the soft, sweet-smelling mist that surrounded her. Wafting upwards, she looked down at her own body below her. She watched the flurry of concerned medics around her lifeless form on the theatre bed.

After three more attempts to shock Maddy into life, the medics gave up.

'Time of death?' the senior medic asked, looking at the wall clock for confirmation.

'Two thirty p.m.,' said one of the team.

Maddy looked on as a young nurse gently pulled the sheet up over her bruised and bloodied face. 'Wait!' she called. 'I'm not sure this is right!'

'Time to inform the family,' said the doctor, removing his latex gloves and making his way towards the operating-room doors.

Maddy floated among the machines, ignored by the medical team. 'Hey, wait! I'm still here. Doesn't anybody see me?'

The young nurse paused for a moment, looking straight through Maddy, before removing the crash cart from the room.

Maddy watched the group of medical staff moving away from her covered body. Nothing made any sense. One moment she was on her way back up the pathway from the beach, the next she was hovering over her own body. 'No, something's not right here. There must be a mistake. I'm not ready to die,' she shouted, but no one heard her.

Maddy followed behind the Spanish doctor, floating through the swing doors, down the corridor and into the main foyer where her family waited.

'I'm so sorry …' the doctor began.

But Maddy had stopped listening. Something felt wrong – incomplete somehow – but she couldn't remember what it was. Looking at the anguished faces around the doctor, she tried to make sense of the scene in front of her. Pippa and Zara stood close to their mother. Maddy absorbed the shuddering sobs that shook Zara's frame as she pulled a wailing Pippa towards her. Maddy moved to gently wipe a tear from Pippa's cheek, and as her ghostly fingers brushed her face, a small hand unknowingly touched hers.

'Oh, my beautiful Pippa,' whispered Maddy, a sense of completeness washing over her. Then she felt herself being pulled tenderly and lifted away. She watched as Zara folded Pippa tightly into her arms, her mouth softly kissing the tears from her face. In the gentle draught, voices called for Maddy to join them.

'I can hear you,' she whispered back. 'It's all ok … I'm ready. I can go with you now,' she murmured to the hazy shapes gathering

around her, allowing herself to drift into the warm draught. 'It's not really so bad,' she sighed, looking back for one last time. Then something caught her eye ... and she remembered.

'No!' she shrieked to the shapes floating around her. 'STOP! I remember ... I can't go yet. I have to stay.' And, in a panic, she did the only thing that was open to her: she dragged herself out of the draught and stepped into Zara.

Chapter 5

As Maddy stepped into Zara's body, Zara felt a strange sensation, not unlike that experienced when a plane drops suddenly from a great height. Her stomach lurched and her legs crumbled beneath her.

'Zara!' exclaimed Gareth, catching her just as her knees met the floor. 'Whoa, darling ... stay with me ... I've got you,' he told her, cradling her trembling body in his arms. Zara felt sick. Not just queasy sick but violently ill. With one hand over her mouth she accepted the disposable grey bowl that was thrust under her chin and retched painfully.

'It's the shock,' said Lisa, taking over from Gareth and pushing a long curl of her daughter's dark hair behind her ear.

Pippa stood nearby, howling with grief, refusing to be comforted by her father as Nathan looked on, white-faced.

'I think ... I'd like to take the girls home now,' said Lisa, haltingly, her face betraying her grief.

Jon looked at his wife, now sitting on the hospital floor alongside an ashen-looking Zara. 'Yes. I think home would be better for everyone. Can you take the girls back?' he asked Gareth. 'I'll stay here with Nathan to handle any necessary paperwork. We'll follow you shortly.' Jon's face looked strained as he checked Nathan was in agreement.

'Is Maddy going to be left here all alone?' cried Pippa, her tanned face now pale under the harsh hospital lights. Lisa hugged her. 'Oh, my darling. Maddy's no longer with us. She's already gone, sweetheart ... she can't feel any pain or loneliness now. I promise.'

Jon looked at his wife. Theology and explaining death were not his forte.

'Can I see her before we go?' Pippa asked.

All eyes turned to Nathan. 'I'll see what I can arrange.'

Gareth looked at Zara. 'Do *you* want to see her?'

Zara paused, taking in the traumatised faces of her mother and sister. 'Yes. I'd like to see her, please.'

Maddy's body had been moved to a small, curtained room. Only her face was visible; her shattered body was covered by a white sheet. There was an eerie silence as the sad group shuffled towards the bed. The medical staff had cleaned away much of the blood from Maddy's face and now the trail of angry cuts and abrasions, evidence of her fall onto the rocks, was clearly visible: the pink puckered tears and pale bruises, a stark contrast to the waxy pallor of her lifeless skin.

'Oh!' moaned Pippa. 'Poor Maddy's face,' she whispered, grabbing her mother's hand tightly. Lisa pulled Pippa towards her. 'She's all right now, darling. She doesn't hurt any longer, I promise,' she said, gently pushing back part of Maddy's fringe and leaning forward to lay a kiss on her forehead. 'She's at peace now, Pippa.'

Zara stood back from the bed, watching from afar. To her, her sister's body looked empty – as if the person inside had simply gone, leaving it like an abandoned shell.

'She's not in there, is she?' Pippa asked in a low voice, looking hard at her beloved mentor, then back to her mother. 'Has she gone to heaven?'

Lisa nodded and hugged the six-year-old. 'Yes, darling, I'm afraid she's left us here and gone on to a much better place.'

Zara approached the bed slowly, looking down at her sister

and best friend with an aching heart. 'Where are you now, Maddy?' she whispered under her breath, touching the white, bloodless lips with her fingertips. 'I know you're not in there, but … I can still feel you with me. Don't leave me, Maddy,' she murmured, her hands trembling with grief and despair.

'I'm close, Zara. Closer than you realise …'

For Maddy, her own death was an unfamiliar concept. She had no idea what was supposed to happen next, nor how she should be feeling, but she was sure that invading a living person's body was not the correct protocol.

Having stepped into Zara, she had no idea how to step out. That being said, the whole dying experience had been traumatic and she had no intention of leaving the safety of Zara's body at the moment, despite the beckoning shapes floating around her.

Surprisingly, there was no sense of overcrowding: as Zara moved, Maddy simply went with her. She watched through her sister's eyes, experiencing her host's emotions, yet still retaining her own.

'Sorry, Zara,' she said. 'I won't hurt you – but I do need to stay here with you for a while. I never knew this was possible, and everything is still a bit hazy, but I know I can't leave yet. I need to remember exactly what happened, and for that I'm going to need time and your help. Then I'll find a way to go … I promise.'

Chapter 6

As if aware of the unfolding tragedy, the Majorcan weather began to change and the skies turned dark grey with thick, ominous clouds. As they drove back along the coastal road, Zara watched the wind-whipped sea frothing and crashing against the headland and the tops of the palm trees bending against the wind.

'Looks like it's going to rain. And hard,' said Gareth, breaking the silence in the car.

Zara shivered, her thin cotton dress now inadequate, as the island's natural bright light began to dim with the gathering clouds. The automatic windscreen wipers had begun their dance against the first raindrops, and their thud-thud kept her black thoughts in check: by concentrating on their mechanical movement, she could keep her mind from its dangerous investigation of the facts. Zara couldn't shake the feeling that there was much more to Maddy's fatal fall than met the eye.

A mobile phone pinged in the back of the car.

'I've got a text from Nathan. Did anyone find Maddy's phone?' asked Lisa.

Zara turned around. 'No. I wasn't looking for it. Wasn't it with her?'

'No. No one's found it. He's asked us to search for it when we get back to the villa.'

'I'll take a look,' said Gareth, happy to have something constructive to do.

Zara turned her attention back to the windscreen wipers.

Something definitely wasn't right. Maddy always had her phone with her. The silence in the car was deafening.

Safe within Zara, Maddy was beginning to remember things, drifting between memories of sunny days, sailing on the bright waters and the darker images linked to her fall. The normal senses of fear or injustice were anchored with the living, not the dead, but Maddy still felt that leaving now would endanger others; she needed to remember why and how she had died, and fast. At first, any recollection to the exact manner of her death was blocked: Spirit's gift of 'bliss' to the departed – no shock, no pain, no traumatic memories; a time in which Spirit allowed individuals to come to terms with their own demise, comforted by the balm of forgetfulness and safe for as long as needed. Only Maddy knew she couldn't stay forever. She'd stayed for a purpose and it had something to do with ... The memory of a familiar face floated tantalisingly out of reach.

Chapter 7

The rain had finally stopped, and Zara, accompanied by Gareth, stepped out onto the patio back at the villa. The sun, as if apologising for its short departure, quickly burnt through the clouds to dry up the surrounding area. Zara lifted a wet towel off one of the sunbeds and dropped it onto a pile of hastily discarded swimwear. Gareth kissed her gently on the cheek then turned towards the pathway. 'Do you want me to come?' Zara asked.

'No, I'm fine. I'll just see if she dropped her phone on the walk down or back up from the beach. And if it's not there, I'll look on her boat.'

Zara looked up as her mother approached, a weary smile playing on her lips.

'Ok?' Lisa asked.

'Not really. How's Pippa?'

'Tucked up in bed. Thought a little rest might help her. Have you found Maddy's phone?'

Zara shook her head. 'No, Gareth's going down now to look for it.'

Lisa surveyed the surrounding property, the dripping trees and damp, steaming grass. 'Can't quite believe what's happened, still such a shock. I feel sick, physically ill at the thought of her lying out there all alone last night.'

Zara too shuddered at the thought. 'How's Jon taking it?' she asked.

'Bravely. He's back now, in the kitchen with Nathan.' Lisa collapsed into a wicker chair, wrapping her thin linen shirt around her shoulders and shivering. 'Nathan's being marvellous, he's handling everything so calmly, but then he would. He's always so extraordinarily helpful. He's organising things with the hospital and the necessary legalities. He tells me the Guardia Civil need to investigate the area around where Maddy fell. Part of me thinks I should take Pippa back home tomorrow, remove her from all of this.'

Zara lifted her face towards her mother. 'It will take time for Pippa to get over this, Mum. Maddy was her world.'

'I know. We all loved Maddy,' Lisa replied, scrabbling for a tissue.

Zara and her mother fell into silence as the sun attempted to drill some warmth into their trembling souls.

Returning from the beach, Gareth looked at both Lisa and Zara, shaking his head. 'No phone that I could see down on the rocks, or along the pathway, but I did find this.' He opened his fist to display a delicate gold ring; two dolphins, beaks and tails entwined, rested in his hand.

Zara picked up the ring from his outstretched palm, turning it around in her fingers. 'She wore this around her neck, on a chain. Where did you find it?' she asked.

'On the edge of the pathway, where she must have fallen. I nearly missed it among the stones.'

Zara smiled. 'She never told me who gave her this ring and what it meant, but I knew it must have been special as she's worn it all of this holiday.'

'Didn't you push her for a name? Do you think he's from here or from home?' asked Lisa.

Zara smiled again at the memory. 'I did, but she just laughed at me – gave me one of those low, throaty giggles and

31

shook her head. I took that as a denial or a "none-of-your-business" gesture. If there was someone, they would have had to be very special; Maddy was in no hurry for a relationship.' She smiled wryly and turned to Gareth. 'Mum's talking about taking Pippa back home tomorrow.'

'Tomorrow? Oh, should we come back with you?' he asked, still visibly shaken by the events of the day. 'Not sure I'm inclined to stay on and celebrate our engagement here under the circumstances.'

'Oh, Zara, Gareth!' Lisa's hand flew to her mouth. 'I'd forgotten you've booked a two-week break in Ibiza. You should go,' she told them, looking from one to the other. 'That's if you feel up to it? I'm not sure that we can take Maddy back to England yet, and then there will be the funeral to organise. Why don't you both go as arranged. Nathan can help me, with Jon.'

Zara looked at Gareth. Their engagement party had been so wonderfully romantic, but now it felt like it had never happened. 'Not sure, Mum. Still in shock, I guess. We'll have a chat about what we want to do later and let you know.'

Lisa nodded. Nobody was thinking straight at the moment.

'I'll go back down to check Maddy's boat for her phone,' said Gareth.

'Do you need any help?' asked Zara, secretly hoping the answer would be no.

'I'd prefer to go on my own, if you don't mind,' answered Gareth. He too had cared deeply for Maddy and hadn't yet had a chance to face his own emotions, let alone cry. He needed some space for his own thoughts. Time away from the family would allow him to grieve in private.

Relieved, Zara answered, 'Fine, I'll go take a shower. I'm feeling very cold.'

Back in their section of the villa, Zara ran the shower on maximum heat and climbed under its welcoming spray. She was physically drained, emotionally spent and cold. Shivering, she allowed the warmth to seep into her bones as she stood, arms stretched wide, hands pressed against the cubicle's vivid blue tiles, allowing the water's force to pummel the back of her neck. Slowly, she could feel her muscles responding and the coil of tightness within her begin to unravel. Dropping her head, she began to cry. 'Oh, Maddy, I'm going to miss you so much.'

Maddy was finding the process of inhabiting Zara's body frustrating. She could see everything through Zara's eyes, hear the conversations around her, but she had no way of making Zara aware of her presence or of mastering the ability to interact. She was beginning to regret her decision to step in. Everything within this body felt unnatural to her. She had no idea what she was doing, hadn't yet remembered why she needed to stay or how she was going to get Zara to help her. And worst of all, she still didn't know how she was going to get out.

Zara wrapped her steaming body in a fresh towel and stood in front of the bathroom mirror, her image blurred by the condensation. She started to clean her teeth. Pausing, her mouth foaming with toothpaste, she looked up at the somehow unfamiliar and hazy reflection staring back at her. Grabbing a hand towel, she wiped the glass clear and peered closer. With her wet, dark hair scraped back, her face looked different; her cheekbones, usually plump and rounded, had a more chiselled appearance and her warm brown eyes looked green under the bathroom light. Zara shuddered, spitting out the toothpaste and pulling back from her reflection. She ran her fingers through her hair, and her curls bounced back, immediately restoring the image to a more familiar one.

'Well, that worked,' realised Maddy. 'You can see me. But your own sense of realism is going to deny I'm here, isn't it? Not that I blame you … not easy being in someone else's body either, Zara. Can you hear me?'

Zara, still shaken, wiped the mirror again and re-examined her reflection. Picking up her hairdryer, she deliberately blew hot air onto the glass before tipping her head forward and finger-drying her hair.

'Obviously not,' groaned Maddy, adding, 'God knows how this is supposed to work.' She chuckled at her own irreverence.

Wandering back into the bedroom, Zara found Gareth resting on the bed.

'Any luck with the phone?' she asked.

Gareth shook his head. 'No, but are you all right? I thought I heard you call out just now?'

Clasping her towel more closely around herself, Zara shuddered. 'I think I must still be in shock, and my imagination is in overdrive. I need a hug,' she replied, climbing up next to Gareth and snuggling into his warm body.

Gareth wrapped her in his arms and kissed her, beginning to stroke and nudge her body beneath the towel. 'Mmm, you smell so good. Don't suppose I can persuade you to roll over onto your back, can I?'

Zara smiled, allowing her tense body to relax under his familiar loving hands, and as he gently moved his body over hers, she felt herself responding to his hardness, opening first her mouth and then her thighs with a small, expectant sigh.

'No!' Maddy shrieked, experiencing a sense of suffocation under the weight.

'No!' Zara cried, pushing Gareth away with a strength that took him completely by surprise. 'Don't touch me,' she cried. Then, realising what she'd done and said, she clamped her hand over her mouth in disbelief.

They faced one another on the bed in shocked silence. Zara held a pillow tightly to her chest, deliberately separating herself from Gareth and providing a degree of modesty.

'I'm so sorry, Zara. I should have known you weren't ready …' he said, his manhood lying like the moment, redundant and spent.

'No, it's not that … it's …' She lowered her eyes, shaking her head in confusion. 'I don't know what it is, but I can't do … that,' she whispered. 'Not at the moment.'

'I understand,' he replied, holding her close to disguise his embarrassment. 'It doesn't matter; it's my fault, insensitive of me. So sorry, Zara. There'll be other times.'

'Not while I'm still in here, there won't,' thought Maddy in panic. *She knew Zara was beginning to sense her. The response to Gareth's lovemaking attempt was proof. Now she needed to understand how she'd managed to do it.*

Mortified by her outburst, Zara lay beside Gareth, the pillow once again jammed between them. Her heart beat fast and her breath was laboured. 'I'm really sorry. I promise that won't happen again,' she told him. 'I just don't know what came over me. I suddenly felt so strange and … frightened.'

'Its fine,' Gareth assured her. 'I understand. It was probably an inappropriate time.' The truth was, Gareth had no idea what was happening. One moment his fiancée was responding to him, and the next, she was violently pushing him away. He'd never experienced such behaviour before from Zara and it left him feeling inadequate and brutish. 'I'll leave you for a few minutes to get dressed and I'll go join the others,' he suggested.

Relieved, Zara nodded. 'I'll be out shortly.'

Later, an emotionally numb Zara stumbled into the living room where Jon and Lisa were talking in hushed voices. Seeing her approach, Nathan signalled to them to shush.

Gareth walked towards Zara, protectively. Taking her hands in his, he smiled sympathetically. He knew what he was about to tell her would destroy her. 'Zara ...' he began, looking back at Nathan for support. 'I'm so sorry, Zara ... but it appears Maddy's death may not have been an accident.'

Chapter 8

Maddy watched their faces through her host's eyes. Drawn to one expression in particular, she began to remember ... how the uneven rocks from the path had hurt her feet, so she'd put her shoes back on as she climbed up the pathway towards the villa. The surrounding shrubbery and trees had created darker sections along the route and she'd felt grateful for the strategically placed lights along the bank. She remembered the rustling she'd heard from the bushes close to the top of the pathway, and then the dark shape that loomed into view, grabbing her wrist and twisting her off her feet. And Maddy remembered the sharp, shooting pain that had travelled up to her armpit, and the smell of his hand as he clamped her mouth shut ...

'What do you mean not an accident?' asked Zara, her heart thumping uncomfortably with a sudden sense of fear, as a nauseating sickness washed through her.

... *Maddy remembered how he'd sniffed her hair, and the deep sigh that bubbled in the back of his throat. Sickening sounds that made her want to gag. As he lifted her off the ground and carried her towards the edge, she had kicked out at him. Then, lowering her onto the uneven ground, he had spun her around to face him, tightening his hold on her arm, sending pain up to her shoulder again.*

Zara unconsciously grasped her shoulder, her eyes wide and questioning as she looked back into Gareth's face.

Maddy recalled the glow from the pathway lights, the look in his eyes as he snapped the delicate chain from around her neck, her gold dolphin ring tumbling down the front of her dress as he half lifted, half dragged her closer to the edge ...

Feeling unsteady, Zara stumbled towards a chair, her arms reaching out. 'What do you mean not an accident?' she whispered again.

... Maddy had known at that point what he intended to do and there was nothing she could do to stop him. He spun her around yet again, pushing her hard on one side of her body, knocking her off-balance. Her shoes caught and twisted as her feet slipped underneath her. As she felt herself falling, she tried to find something to grab onto, clutching only thin air. She saw that there was nothing below her to break her fall. When she hit the rocks, she knew that was the end; every part of her body felt broken. No one would find her until the morning.

'What are you saying?' Zara asked, her sense of fear increasing with each moment.

Gareth bent down onto his knees beside her and took her shaking hands in his. 'Maddy may have intended ...' he began, unable to finish as he watched the colour drain from Zara's face. 'We believe ...' he tried again, unsuccessfully.

'That she deliberately took her own life,' finished Jon.

'No!' Maddy screamed.

The words punched through Zara. '*Deliberately*?' she challenged. 'I don't understand?' Zara looked from one face to the other, her mouth suddenly dry. 'Deliberately? What are you telling me?'

'We found a note ...' began Lisa, looking around for support. Nathan shuffled uncomfortably, watching Jon's face.

'What note?' Zara asked, her face now visibly etched with fear.

'Her note ... addressed to you,' Lisa whispered.

'To me? From Maddy? Where?'

'In her bedside table,' replied a nervous Lisa.

'Ah!' breathed Maddy. 'My note ...'

'Who found it?' asked Zara.

'Jon did. He was looking for Maddy's phone,' said Lisa. Her face was white and pinched, and she clasped a tissue tightly in her right hand. 'We opened it. I'm sorry, I know it was addressed to you, but ...'

Zara looked at all four faces watching her as she took the opened envelope from her mother.

'I'm sorry,' Lisa murmured again, racked with guilt and embarrassment.

'Why didn't you let me see it first?' Zara whimpered, unhappily shaking her head.

Lisa glanced furtively at Nathan and Jon again. 'We were looking for answers.'

'You should have given it to me first,' Zara muttered as fresh tears slipped down her face at the sight of Maddy's familiar handwriting.

The room fell silent as she read:

Dear Zara,

By the time you receive this I will have already gone. I'm so sorry it had to be this way, but I couldn't pretend any longer and this felt like the only option left for me. I realise my actions will be called selfish, but love and shame are powerful emotions. I've hidden the truth for so long and I wasn't sure you'd understand. I know in time you'll forgive me, everyone will. I never intended to hurt anyone, but my unhappiness has become too much to bear and in the end, I had no choice. I will always love you. You will always be my best friend. Your loving sister, Maddy

Zara looked up at her mother, who had collapsed sobbing into Jon's arms. Silently, she passed the note over to Gareth.

'We believe this letter to you was her suicide note,' Jon said, his voice surprisingly controlled for a man who'd just lost his daughter.

'No,' hissed Maddy.

'No, I don't believe it,' said Zara, shaking her head. 'This is not a suicide note. I know Maddy. It must mean something else. She loved life; she loved us – she wouldn't commit suicide. There must be another explanation.'

Gareth looked around uncomfortably as he passed the note back to Zara. Then, standing, he took a position in line with the others. 'It does sound like one, darling,' he told her.

Zara battled with conflicting emotions – anger that they'd opened her letter and disbelief at the contents. 'Do you think this is a suicide note?' she asked Nathan, looking for the opinion of a professional.

Nathan cautiously nodded his head. 'I think ... it's possible.'

Zara took time to think before answering: 'Then I suppose it will have to be given to the Guardia Civil and those carrying out the autopsy, so they can record her death as suicide.' Standing up, she carefully folded the note back into its envelope.

Gareth watched Zara's shoulders heave with emotion and placed his arms around her shaking frame.

Nathan glanced in Jon's direction and was met with a stony stare. 'I'm hoping Maddy's death will be recorded as an accidental fall,' he ventured, looking at Jon again. 'Suicide is always difficult to prove – that's unless they find a high level of drugs or alcohol in her system that could point to an attempted suicide, or ... if there's a history of depression or previous attempts.'

'Well that's a "no",' replied Zara, still in disbelief. 'Maddy never suffered from depression.'

At first, Nathan appeared to stall over a response, then, catching Jon's eye, he continued. 'I'm afraid, Zara, the truth is that Maddy did have some difficulties when she was young.'

'What kind of difficulties?' asked Lisa, as shocked as Zara.

Jon measured the looks of incredulity on the surrounding faces. 'Nathan had to put Maddy on antidepressants,' he told them.

'But why?' asked Zara, shocked. 'When? She never told me any of this.'

'It was after the death of a close friend—' began Nathan.

'What friend?' asked Zara. 'I never knew about this.'

All heads turned towards Jon and Nathan.

'That was another tragedy,' said Jon, shaking his head sadly. 'Young chap, aged fifteen or thereabouts, I think. Brother of one of Maddy's girlfriends. They found him hanging from a tree on Wimbledon Common, not far from our house. He obviously spent some time with Maddy when they were growing up. I knew him "professionally" for a summer as his parents sent him to me for clinical help. His suicide came as a shock to everyone. And Maddy took it all very badly. Not long after that, I sent her to Spain – a different environment, a chance to change her outlook on life. That's where she discovered her love of the sea and a passion for sailing.' Jon smiled back at the watching faces, then added, 'Patrick was another waste of a promising life.'

Lisa patted her husband's arm affectionately. 'Maddy was a lucky girl to have a father like you; many parents don't understand their children and would have just given up on a troubled teenager. You probably saved her back then.'

Jon looked down at his wife's adoring face. 'Maddy was my blood, Lisa, my daughter. I'll do anything to protect *my* blood.' Watching the slight drop of her shoulders, he added quickly, 'And *my* family.'

Lisa nodded, pulling him closer.

Zara was still unconvinced. 'I'm sorry, but I'm still finding this all too unbelievable. Just because she took some antidepressants as a teenager doesn't mean she had suicidal tendencies. I know there were some things she never talked about, things she hid from me ... but to want to kill herself?'

Lisa moved towards her daughter, holding her close. 'I think there are many things we didn't understand about our Maddy. Her note to you does seem to suggest she wanted to—'

'No!' Zara interrupted, pulling away from her mother. 'Maddy wouldn't commit suicide. There has to be another explanation,' she insisted, dodging Gareth's outstretched hand. 'No, I'm not accepting that. She had so much to live for. What about the offer from the hotel here in Majorca? They wanted her to take guests out sailing next summer, even teach.'

Lisa looked at Jon. 'I didn't know about that.'

'She was so excited about it,' continued Zara. 'And what about the mysterious person she spoke to on the phone, whenever she thought no one was within earshot. She was happier over the last few months than I've ever seen her.'

'Perhaps something went wrong with this mysterious person?' suggested Lisa, with kindness.

'Even if that's true, Maddy wouldn't do that. She wasn't a quitter,' Zara argued.

Jon moved purposefully across the room to face Zara, his expression unreadable. 'What we've discussed needs to be between us only. We do not *want* a suicide label on Maddy's death; we owe it to her to protect her reputation. It will be better that way.' The tone of his voice cut through the emotional shock, silencing everyone. 'We've all read the contents of this note,' he went on, removing it from Zara's trembling hand, 'and can form our own opinions. It should now be destroyed.'

Zara felt her stomach tighten as an unexplained and sudden sense of terror took control of her body.

'The coroners can draw their own conclusions too, without any help from us,' Jon continued. 'Maddy's *fall* should be referred to as a tragic accident, nothing more. I want assurances from you all that this is the line this family will take. We've all suffered enough. Let us at least keep some dignity.'

There was a pause as he scanned their faces. Looking in Nathan's direction, he waited. 'Are *you* in agreement with me?' he asked.

Nodding, Nathan turned to a distraught and frightened-looking Zara. 'An accident finding is better for Maddy. I think Jon's suggestion is best for all concerned,' he offered gently.

The room fell silent except for the ticking of an old clock over the fireplace.

'I agree not to mention her note,' said Gareth. 'Best to call it an accident,' he added, taking Zara's hand.

Zara looked at Gareth first, then at her mother.

Blowing her nose, Lisa nodded. 'Me too,' she said.

'Zara?' Jon asked, his chin raised as he watched her, his dark eyes unwavering, their unspoken message clear.

Zara's body began to tremble again as her shoulders slumped in submission. A clear voice in her head cut through her thoughts.

'Not true!' it shouted.

Zara's eyes flew wide open as they darted around the room.

'Zara, it's me ... you can hear me, can't you?'

Zara screwed her eyes shut, but the voice in her head continued.

'I know it's frightening for you, but believe me, it's more frightening for me. I need your help. I'm sorry to do this, but I have no idea of how long I can stay here, so I need you to listen.'

Gareth watched Zara anxiously as she fought to shut out this inner voice.

'Zara!' repeated Jon.

Her head snapped back to attention as Jon's voice cut through the internal buzzing.

'Are we clear, Zara?'

'Zara, I didn't jump and I didn't fall. I need your help. Listen to me—'

'Yes. Very clear, I understand,' she replied, shutting down the small inner voice as she answered. Her sad eyes lowered and locked onto her clasped hands.

'Good, then that's final. We will no longer speak of the *suicide* matter.' And, walking away from the group, Jon waved for Nathan to join him in his study.

Once again, there was silence, except for the ticking of the clock.

'Shall we have something to drink?' Gareth's voice broke the awkward hush. 'I know I could do with a strong one. Who's with me?' he asked, wringing his hands, clearly feeling uncomfortable following the most recent revelation.

Lisa and Zara nodded in agreement. 'I'll just go check on Pippa,' said Lisa, tucking a loose curl behind her ear and stuffing her spent tissues deep into her pockets. Gareth watched her leave then walked over to the drinks tray where he picked up a bottle of gin. He poured Zara a generous measure with a splash of tonic, then placed the glass into her shaking hands.

Lifting her head, Zara smiled weakly at Gareth, grateful for the alcohol. She tipped her head back and swallowed the contents of the glass in their entirety with relief.

'Better?' he asked, his brow furrowed with concern.

'Zara!' Maddy called from within her. 'Don't drink alcohol, it blocks me out.'

Zara nodded. 'Yes, better,' she said, offering her glass for a refill. Then, deliberately taking another large gulp, she silenced Maddy's voice.

Chapter 9

Early the following morning, having slept very badly, Nathan Collins threw his bag into the car. Lifting his arm, he waved goodbye to Lisa and Jon. He liked Lisa. He'd liked Tilly too, but that had also ended in tragedy. He thought them both good women and good mothers. Looking at Lisa now, he felt that familiar sickening sense of guilt. Why had he allowed things to go so far? Now it was all unravelling, all too late.

Jon pulled away from his wife and approached Nathan, placing one arm over his shoulder. Then he patted him on the back and uttered those familiar words: 'Remember, Nathan, the secret of enjoyment for everyone is to ensure there is no mess at the end.' Nathan felt nauseous as he recalled the image of a broken Maddy lying on the rocks. 'We'll all get through this,' Jon told him. 'And don't forget,' he added, hugging him briefly as he whispered in his ear, 'the three wise monkeys.'

Nathan drew away from Jon's embrace, nodding his head in resignation. He knew why he'd allowed it to continue; he'd had no choice.

Nathan's mind drifted back to all those years ago, when, as a young man, he'd made a stupid mistake – a mistake that led to a terrible tragedy. That secret had ruined more than one life and bound him to Jon for eternity.

Driving away from the Pink Villa towards Palma Airport, Nathan had time to reflect on the number of messes he'd been asked to clear up for Jon. Too many and all wrong. Drawing nearer to the airport, Nathan shuddered as a pain shot through his ribcage. 'Not now, for God's sake,' he whispered through gritted teeth, patting his front jacket pocket to check for his pills. 'I can't leave this mess as it is. I owe it to Maddy.' Seeing the sign for the airport, Nathan turned off onto the slip road, and made for the car-hire drop-off and his plane to England.

Chapter 10

Maddy was experimenting with ways to reach Zara. She knew that her own feelings of shock and revulsion were getting through to her; that was obvious from the way she'd pushed poor Gareth off. Now she needed to transfer her thoughts into Zara's head too. Maddy's memory still only recalled jumbled images. Zara would have to work out what these meant. For Zara to help, she had to see things through Maddy's eyes.

It was dark when Zara and Gareth reached the spot where Maddy had fallen. Standing there in the light breeze, they looked out across the bay. A web of plastic police tape stretched ominously across the area where she had fallen. Zara looked down. The torrential rain had washed the surrounding area and cleaned away any traces of blood from the rocks below. The line of strategically spaced lights lit the walkway down to the beach and jetty, and the full moon reflected off the thickening grey sea. Everything was as it was, only now everything had changed.

'She loved this place so much,' said Zara. 'Did you know the villa once belonged to her grandmother, Abigail? That's why it's called the Pink Villa; it was her favourite colour. Maddy told me she intended to live here when working in Majorca. She wanted to run her sailing-school business from here.'

'Did Lisa know that?' Gareth asked in surprise.

'I don't know. Maddy told me the villa would be hers when she reached twenty-five, and I'm sure Mum knew that. But the sailing business was a new idea. She wanted to create something different for young people to experience on the water. She referred to it as a "form of healing", using the sea and the elements to repair the body, mind and soul. For her, the water provided a safe place to "find herself". She wanted to encourage troubled teenagers to work through their issues out on the water, learning to function with and trust others, helping them to find their own inner strength and peace. She had plans for turning the whole house into a private hotel.'

'Really?'

'A retreat, she called it.'

'Oh, I'm not sure Lisa would have agreed to that. What would happen to Lisa and Jon's holidays if she had done that?' asked Gareth.

'I suppose they'd come down and stay as normal, but use the guest house and share the place with her paying guests. The villa's large enough.'

'I don't think Lisa knew about Maddy owning the villa, or her plans, Zara. Your mother told me she was flying over an interior decorator to do the place up in the autumn.'

'Ah. Well, she can do what she wants now. Maddy won't need it,' said Zara sadly, shaking her head. 'This is the one place where she was so happy; so many plans for the future, all involving the Pink Villa. She used to say it was here that she felt at peace with herself. She loved this villa and she loved the sea. That's why I still don't accept what they're asking me to believe. If she really intended to take her own life, she'd have just sailed off into the sunset and dropped into the sea. She was never afraid of the water. But here?' Zara paused, looking back down at the lethal rocks. 'It just doesn't feel right.'

'Then maybe it really was a fall? A terrible accident, after all,' suggested Gareth.

'It still doesn't make any sense. How could she have fallen? We all knew how dangerous the path was; we all knew to walk close to the lights, not the edge. Maddy was like a mountain goat. She knew these steep pathways. She could walk them in her sleep.'

'Maybe she'd drunk too much at the party and stumbled?'

'Unlikely. Maddy didn't drink much. She hated to be out of control.'

'The autopsy will check for alcohol or drugs in her blood.'

'I know. But they won't find anything. And I still don't believe she took her own life, whatever Jon and Mum tell me.'

'And the note?'

Zara paused as confused images tumbled around her head.

'She talked about leaving,' he reminded her.

Zara turned to face Gareth. 'No, she said, "I will have already gone."' That could mean she was off on a trip. The note was found in a drawer – why wasn't it left for me in my room? Who's to say she wasn't going off somewhere and didn't want me to stop her?' Zara watched Gareth's face closely as he absorbed her comments. He, like the others, didn't really know or understand Maddy. 'No. If Maddy intended to end her life, she would have taken the *Phoenix* out to sea and done it there, not here. Not so public. And not for Pippa to witness. You know how protective she was of Pippa.'

Gareth felt a twinge of unease. 'So, what are you saying?'

Zara stood watching the gentle swell against the surrounding coastline. 'I don't know. I just believe something happened here; something that wasn't just an accident.'

'Nathan said the police and the Guardia Civil have measured the surrounding area, taking the position and the angle of her fall. They're still working on the theory of an accident.'

Zara said nothing as an image of dark eyes flashed into her head.

'We want an accident ruling, don't we?' Gareth asked.

Zara lifted her face to his. 'That's what Nathan and Jon want,' she snorted. Then she saw an image of Maddy lying on the rocks below and felt something move behind her. Turning quickly, she sensed a push to one side of her body and, grabbing onto Gareth's arm, she stumbled.

'Zara!' Gareth caught her below the elbow. 'Careful! We don't want another accident. The plastic incident ribbons shuddered as Zara's hand brushed across them. 'Let's move back, shall we?' he suggested, unnerved.

Walking up towards the manicured gardens, Zara stopped. 'Shh,' she whispered.

'What?' he asked, the hairs on the back of his neck tingling.

'I thought I heard something.'

'Where?'

'In the bushes, up there. Look!' Zara pointed to a large shrub ahead and to the right of them.

'There's no one here, Zara. Just us.'

But for that moment, the image of a figure, furtively creeping above them in the undergrowth, seemed so real to Zara.

'Could there have been someone else out here on that night? Someone who startled Maddy and made her lose her footing?' she asked.

Gareth listened to Zara's suggestion. 'Possibly. But if so, why didn't they run for help?'

'Unless, they wanted her to fall? Or it was … a deliberate push.'

'What do you mean "push"?'

'Just now, I sensed something "push" into me. I know it sounds improbable, but it felt so … real.'

'Now you're beginning to freak me out, Zara. You'll be telling me next you can see Maddy at the villa.'

'No. Not see her … but I do *feel* her sometimes. She's definitely somewhere close by.'

*'Closer than you think. Keep on this train of thought, Zara. I'm
trying my hardest to connect.'*

'That's it,' said Gareth, bristling in fright. 'We're going back
to England on the next flight. We need to leave this place and
let the authorities deal with Maddy's death. They're trained
to see the whole picture objectively. We're all too emotionally
connected and I don't like this talk of ghosts. You know that.'

Zara shook her head sadly. 'Something is telling me Maddy
didn't want to die. She had too much to live for. I need to find
the truth, Gareth. Whatever the autopsy gives as a reason for
her death, I believe there is something we've not considered.'

'Like what?'

'I don't know. There's just something inside me that won't
accept what we are being asked to accept. Suicide or accident?
Something doesn't feel right. There's more to this than meets
the eye.'

'Good girl!' encouraged Maddy.

Putting his hands on Zara's shoulders, Gareth looked
deeply into her eyes. 'Zara, we have to accept the simple truth.
Maddy is dead. She wrote you a note – a note that suggested
she intended to kill herself. We've all agreed to say her fall was
an accident, not deliberate. We need to go home to England,
wait for the autopsy report, bury Maddy, mourn for her and
hopefully get on with our lives. We have a wedding to organise
for next year or have you forgotten?'

Zara looked up at Gareth's anguished face. 'I know I'm
being unreasonable, but I can't help it. I loved her so much.
It's like a light's been extinguished before its time and I need
to know why.'

Taking her in his arms, Gareth kissed her head. 'Life has no rhyme or reason sometimes, Zara. We just have to make the best of it.'

Hand in hand, they walked back to the villa.

'Wait!' Zara stopped, pulling at Gareth's hand. 'She never wrote a note for Pippa!'

Gareth looked at Zara closely.

'Or asked me to look out for her.' Zara's face lit up with sudden realisation and hope. 'If she'd meant to take her own life, she would have asked me to look after Pippa,' she added, searching Gareth's face for some sign of agreement.

A sense of unease came over Gareth as he led Zara, weeping, back into their room. Just now, he couldn't find a suitable answer.

Chapter 11

Because the circumstances of Maddy's death were unusual, the examining magistrate required a post-mortem. The autopsy findings for Maddy's demise were recorded as 'death due to blunt force trauma; caused by an accidental fall'. The toxicology report showed a small amount of alcohol in her system, and listed what she'd eaten that day. Nathan had been called to provide information regarding Maddy's general health and medical background. He told them what they needed to know. Working with the British Consul, Nathan obtained all the necessary authorisation for the release and repatriation of Maddy's body, and Nathan and Jon flew back to Majorca to accompany it. For Jon, it gave him another chance to search the property for Maddy's missing mobile phone. His hunt was unsuccessful. For Nathan, ensuring Maddy's safe return was just one more job, one more request from Jon to clean up the more unpleasant things in his life.

There was no pomp or ceremony to greet Maddy as her casket touched down on Gatwick Airport's tarmac, just the necessary ground crew and the undertakers. Maddy wouldn't have cared. She wasn't in there, anyway.

Down on the Majorcan beach, below the villa, a young woman, tiny, tanned and dressed in cut-off denim shorts and a soft, white smocked shirt, furtively climbed up the pathway to the garden. She paused at the police-incident ribbon, touching the overstretched plastic before continuing onto the grass. Here, she stood silently, scanning the magnificent property's shuttered windows for signs of life. Behind her, the dropping sun coloured the granite rocks pink, casting dark, cool shadows onto the house and garden. Barefoot, she cautiously trod the coarse grass, her glossy pink toenails burying themselves among the green blades. As she reached the raised patio, she stopped. Here, holding her breath, she watched the bright bubbles from the pool filter sparkle and dance, leaping momentarily above the darker, still water which reflected the deep blue of the pool tiles. She noticed the abandoned bathrobe, once a soft, fluffy white, now stiff and a shade of sun-bleached cream. Tiptoeing across the patio, she tried the doors, rattling the handles. They were all locked. She moved quickly and delicately, showing her years of training as a dancer, ready to react instantly to any sudden noise or danger.

Lifting her exquisite face towards the dying sun, she closed her eyes, her dark lashes catching the silent tears that tracked her delicate features. Her long, black hair skimmed her shoulder blades as it bounced and curled in the warm evening breeze. Opening her eyes wide, she acknowledged the lone gull that swooped and dived out towards the ocean, its melancholy cry echoing that within her own heart. Her hauntingly sad eyes, sea-green with burnt amber and gold, flashed a look of pain as the bird dropped out of sight. With her hands pressed together as if in prayer, she waited a moment before running silently towards the stone garden balcony, a glint from something gold flashing around her neck as she dropped onto the pathway and down to the beach and the ocean below.

A bearded man waited patiently for her return. As she climbed back into the dinghy, she took one more look up at the rocky pathway then settled herself down in the bow, her delicate fingers grasping the gold circle that hung around her neck. As the boat swung out from the jetty and back out towards the sea, its name, the *Water Hawk*, was clearly visible.

Chapter 12

On the day of Maddy's funeral, it poured with rain. Zara felt a sense of heightened tension and her body was jumpy. Maddy was being buried beside her mother, Matilda Stone, in the local churchyard. The mourners huddled under large black umbrellas that reminded Zara of swooping crows.

Pippa, pale-faced and tiny, dressed in sombre navy, stood to attention, her hand firmly grasped by her mother's. It was she who placed the last white rose on Maddy's casket, and as the bud softly hit the wood, Zara caught her breath.

'I'm here, my darling Pippa. I can still see you.'

'Bye bye, Maddy. I will always love you,' said Pippa, moving away from the lowered casket and back to the security of Lisa.

'And I will love you forever and ever,' Maddy answered.

The congregation began to make their sad way back to Jon and Lisa's home for refreshments, but Zara hovered at the graveside. Gareth, lost within his own thoughts, stood behind her.

'I do understand how you must feel, Zara. I know how much you loved her. It's been a terrible shock for everyone, and it's going to take time to accept.'

Zara looked up at his handsome face with guilt. Since that disastrous attempt at lovemaking, Gareth had not asked again.

'Let's take each day at a time, shall we?' he suggested, smiling at her tear-stained face and gently tucking his hand into hers.

'I'm so sorry.' Zara smiled back. 'I know I'm being irrational, but right now I need someone to say they understand

and give me time to work through this. I can't even understand myself at the moment. I've never felt so confused.'

'We've all been affected by Maddy's death, Zara, but we will get there. As I said, we just need time.'

Safe in his arms, Zara wondered if that would ever be true.

Back at the house, Zara couldn't help but notice the hostility between Lisa and Jon. Upset herself, she avoided it by wandering upstairs to her bedroom, where she kicked off her dark heeled shoes and dumped her handbag on the bed. As she sauntered into her en-suite bathroom, she smelled the scent of coconut oil and jasmine, and opening the mirrored cabinet, she found a fresh circle of milled guest soap left there by the cleaner. 'Ah, so that's what smells of coconut. You loved this smell, didn't you, Maddy?' said Zara, inhaling the soap before carefully placing it back where she'd found it.

'Yes. Reminded me of safe summer days and white sand.'

Zara closed the mirrored door, noting the dark shadows under her eyes. 'Oh, God, I do look a mess,' she told her reflection, moving away too quickly for Maddy to make an appearance.

The sound of voices and the front doorbell drifted upstairs. Zara couldn't face people today. She knew she should, but everything felt too raw. She just couldn't bring herself to smile and nod at the well-meant pity and sympathy. Many of Jon's old friends and clients compared the tragedy of Maddy's accident to the death of her mother, Tilly, and the main sympathy was directed at Jon exclusively. Jon wore tragedy well. It fitted his persona of the wounded but enduring man. Lisa was just the second wife. And as Zara had less status within the family, she felt justified in staying upstairs. Pippa, being a small child, was automatically excused.

Zara had wanted to cry at the churchyard. Really cry. And not the polite kind – the unflattering, hiccupping type of crying, accompanied by huge, noisy gasps of air that left you snotty-nosed and red-eyed, the kind you can only get away with in private. Only now, even alone in her room, it was still difficult. Someone might hear her. Instead, she sniffed loudly, sucking in gulps of air, wiping the fresh tears with torn pieces of toilet paper from the spare roll that was discreetly hidden under a lacy 'hat'. Zara smiled through her tears as she shredded the soggy paper. Maddy would have hated that crocheted hat!

Leaving her own room, Zara quietly opened Maddy's bedroom door, finding Pippa curled up on the bed.

'Hello, darling,' she whispered, sitting down beside her. 'Can I join you?'

Pippa rolled into Zara's lap. 'I miss her so much,' she said as warm, fat tears slipped down onto Zara's arm.

'I know. I do too, darling.' Zara pulled Pippa into her arms and lay beside her, rocking her gently, the comfort and warmth of their united bodies lulling them to sleep.

Maddy could feel both Zara's and Pippa's heartbeats as they lay beside one another. 'Keep Pippa safe, Zara,' she implored.

The sound of footsteps outside the door woke Zara, and she drew Pippa closer as she listened.

'Pippa? Zara? Are you in there?' Jon called through the closed door.

'Ssh … say nothing,' whispered Maddy.

Pippa slept on, one arm thrown carelessly across the pillow, unaware of anyone outside the room. Zara remained perfectly still, holding her breath until the footsteps receded. Looking down at Pippa's small face next to hers, she gently pushed back a tendril of damp hair from her forehead. Pippa stirred, opened her eyes and looked directly at Zara.

'I had a dream that Maddy was lying next to me. I could even feel her breath in my hair.'

'I am here, my sweetheart. It's me beside you,' cooed Maddy with love.

Zara smiled. 'I feel she's here too, sweetheart. And why not? She loved us both very much.'

'Never far, my darlings.'

Footsteps again, only this time faster and lighter. Lisa tapped on the door.

'Zara, darling, could you come down, please?'

Zara slipped off the bed, tucking the covers around Pippa. 'Snooze on, sweetie. I'll be back soon,' she said, then crept out of the bedroom, pulling the door shut behind her.

Lisa looked terrible, her hair dishevelled, her eyelashes clogged with clumps of black mascara and her eyes red from crying. The quick smile she gave Zara looked out of place on her strained face.

'What's happened, Mum?' asked Zara with concern.

There was a pause as a sob caught in Lisa's throat and her hand flew to her mouth.

'Is it about Maddy?' Zara whispered, moving away from the bedroom door.

'Yes,' replied Lisa. 'The lawyers need to speak to us all.'

'About what?' asked Zara, sensing something was more than wrong.

Lisa looked distraught. 'Legal matters.'

'Who's still here?' asked Zara, her stomach now turning with anxiety.

'Only the family and the lawyers ... and Nathan, of course.'

A sense of dread fell over Zara as she reluctantly followed her mother down the stairs.

Chapter 13

From the moment she first met her future son-in-law, Jon Stone, Maddy's grandmother, Abigail Erskine, took an instant dislike to him. Despite his professional qualifications and revered standing within psychiatry circles, there was something about him that she didn't like, or trust. However, aware of her daughter Matilda's determination to marry him, Abigail did all she could to protect Tilly and the family's money from being squandered through what she saw as Jon's lavish and questionable lifestyle. On advice from her faithful family lawyers, she created a number of complicated trusts, appointing her solicitors as the trustees, ensuring that on her death, her sizeable fortune would be carefully protected for the benefit of her grandchildren and subsequent heirs.

On her marriage to Jon, Tilly received a generous monthly allowance from the trustees and the lifetime rights to the use of a property of her choice from the Erskine's Estate Property portfolio. Tilly and Jon chose to occupy Ivy Manor in leafy Wimbledon, a large Edwardian property with a walled and gated courtyard, the perfect setting for a prestigious home and a private psychiatry practice. With the help of creative designers, Tilly fashioned a home that fulfilled all their personal dreams and future needs.

A section of the ground floor, divided off from the main entrance hall, was dedicated to Jon's practice. Separate from the main house, with its own private entrance, it afforded Jon's clients privacy at all times. Designed to create a sense of relaxation and comfort, there was a private consulting office and a room with a daybed and en-suite shower room. The walls had been soundproofed, and no expense spared on the state-of-the-art computer, television and surround-sound hi-fi system. The architects had cleverly created a concealed connecting door from the foyer of the main house into Jon's office. This was locked at all times and for Jon's use only. On some evenings, when Jon was working late or had a tricky case to research, he would remain in his section of the house, sleeping in his 'den', as he called it, so as to avoid waking the rest of the household when he came to bed. On those evenings he took full advantage of his wide screen and surround sound, knowing he disturbed no one.

When Tilly became pregnant, Abigail was ecstatic, prevailing on her trustees to give her daughter lifetime use of the Pink Villa in southern Majorca. She still distrusted Jon but wanted her grandchildren to grow up near water and learn how to sail – a pleasure she had enjoyed as a young woman herself. Fully aware of his mother-in-law's fortune, and her dislike of him, Jon did everything he could to prove himself worthy and a good provider for his own family.

Abigail knew that her daughter and husband lived well above their means; she also had her suspicions that Tilly paid off a great deal of their purchases with her own allowance. But thanks to her lawyer's judiciousness, Abigail knew that both the Erskine properties, Wimbledon and Majorca, remained safely in trust for Tilly's child or children, and their children, in turn. She thought she had secured their future, but she could not have foreseen Tilly's early death. Madeline would be her only grandchild.

As Maddy was too young to inherit on her mother's death, the properties remained in trust, and Jon, as Tilly's widower, was given continuation of the residential rights for both

Wimbledon and Majorca by the trustees. Once Maddy reached the age of twenty-five she would have access to the properties herself. The trust also provided all the necessary funds for her education and upbringing. A housekeeper was found and installed to run the home in Wimbledon and to assist Jon with the task of caring for a small child, all funded by the Erskine fortune.

Abigail was grief-stricken by the fact she had outlived her own daughter and suffered a mild stroke shortly after Tilly's death. Frightened by the consequences of her inevitable demise, with the help of the family lawyers, she again ensured her granddaughter's fortune was safe, handing the management of the trust over to them to oversee. As her frailty increased, so did her lack of mobility, but her mind remained ever sharp. Selling her home, she transferred funds into another trust and moved herself into a private residential home where she lived out her days in relative comfort, visited often by her lawyers, Ernest and Michael Somes, and her granddaughter, Maddy.

Abigail died quietly in her sleep when Maddy was five. It had been her wish to be buried beside her daughter Matilda. 'Place me close, we have lots to talk about. She won't mind the upheaval!' she had told Ernest. 'Although she deserves some, leaving me like she did.' Her funeral was a simple, sombre affair. She wanted neither mourners nor a wake; not even her precious and much-loved Maddy was allowed to attend. 'Burial grounds are too depressing and not the place for a child,' had been her instructions prior to her death. True to her wishes, Maddy did not attend, but many months later, once the ground had healed and the spring flowers had burst through their winter confines, Abigail's faithful housekeeper took Maddy to place fresh flowers on both her mother's and grandmother's graves. Too young to really understand, she happily arranged the blooms in their concrete containers, blue for Mummy and pink for Nana. 'Pink was Nana's favourite colour,' she had advised. When Jon found out about the visit to the churchyard, he took steps to replace Abigail's choice of housekeeper. Now his mother-in-law was dead, he could hire and fire whoever he wished. The estate would pick up all the costs.

As Maddy grew up, the Erskine Trust, managed by Ernest Somes' son, Michael, continued to financially support her and maintain both the Erskine properties. The choice of school was Jon's decision, but the cost was always covered by the estate. There were a number of housekeepers and nannies, varying in age, suitability and length of stay. Jon always interviewed and selected these women; they were expected to run the home, cook the meals and provide support to Jon whenever required. They never lived in, except for babysitting requirements over a business trip. Jon preferred to be a hands-on father and he didn't like other people in the house at night time. As Maddy grew, the babysitting needs lessened, and when she went to school only after-school care was required, so the nannies were dispensed with as Jon worked from home.

When Maddy reached the age of twenty-one, as per her grandmother's wishes and outside of the trust, she received a large lump sum of cash and part of her grandmother's jewellery inheritance. Using some of the money, she bought her own sailing boat, the *Phoenix*. Abigail would have approved of that purchase. All the remaining Erskine fortune and property rights would have become Maddy's fully at the age of twenty-five.

With Maddy's sudden death and no siblings or heir, the Erskine Trust assets would now revert back to the trust to be shared by a number of charities, selected and named by Abigail prior to her own death, to cover such eventualities.

Poor Lisa Stone had no idea that the properties she currently inhabited in both Wimbledon and Majorca were not Jon's, or that they belonged to a trust. Nor was she aware that Maddy was the sole beneficiary of the Erskine estate. While Maddy was alive, providing Maddy was in agreement, Jon could claim the rights to a lifetime use of these properties and any expenses incurred. Now she was dead, there would be a problem ... unless he used his trump card.

On Tilly's death, Jon became fully aware of the draconian rules of inheritance regarding the Erskine Trust's funds. Now, with the death of his daughter Maddy, he was entitled to nothing as Tilly's widower; only Maddy's direct descendants would have had any rights to her grandmother's fortune. Jon realised that now was the time for his big disclosure, a confession that would without doubt prove unpalatable to his family.

Knowing that this revelation was potentially as dangerous as it was valuable, he'd discussed the matter in full with his lawyers. Their advice was to break the news sooner rather than later, and to expect some unpleasantness. The days leading up to Maddy's funeral had therefore been uneasy ones for Jon. He knew he had to share sensitive information with his wife – before she learnt it from a lawyer. He chose his moment just after Maddy had been laid to rest.

Chapter 14

Zara followed her mother into the drawing room, where a fire had been lit. Despite this, the room felt noticeably chilly and she shivered. Jon stood beside his lawyer, Archibold Simpson, to one side of the room. As Lisa entered, Nathan made a move towards her, but she deflected it, taking Zara to the closest settee to sit with her. Thrusting a large gin and tonic into Zara's hand, Gareth sat beside them. The atmosphere felt charged and Zara, holding tightly onto her glass, felt a sense of dread.

Archibold broke the tense silence in the room. 'Jon has asked me to be present today at the reading of Madeline Stone's will,' he began. 'It is not normal practice, but under the circumstances it is a prudent call. It is also vital we understand that for Maddy, her grandmother's wishes were of great importance and with this in mind, she had made arrangements for the eventuality of her own death.'

Maddy stirred within Zara. She could feel the surrounding tension. She had an idea of what they might reveal but was, again, powerless to ensure it would be the truth.

Zara watched the faces around her. Nathan looked worried, Jon resigned and her mother emotionally broken. *Oh my God, what am I going to learn?* she thought, as she sat back against the overfilled cushions, her heart bumping in her chest.

'Before we hear from Maddy's lawyer, perhaps this might be the right time for an explanation,' Jon's lawyer continued, looking over at his client, who waved an acknowledgment of his approval in his direction. Coughing politely, he began: 'For some of you, what I'm about to tell you may come as a surprise or shock. However, I can assure you it is the *truth*, and we have the necessary proof to substantiate it.'

Maddy's lawyer nodded in agreement.

'While still in her early teens, Madeline Stone fell pregnant.'

There was a faint intake of breath from Zara, and Archibold paused as he waited for his words to register. He then continued, 'Her father, Jon, with the assistance of Nathan Collins, her doctor, arranged for Maddy to have her baby in secret in Spain.'

Nathan shivered. He remembered that call from Jon, asking him to examine Maddy. She'd been fourteen at the time, still the small, quiet and serious child that he remembered, but three months pregnant. He thought also of the desk in his surgery in Cuckfield where a silver model of the three wise monkeys sat – a sinister gift from Jon to remind him of their pact, and to keep him walking that tightrope between his Hippocratic Oath and his fear of the law. Coerced, he'd made arrangements to take Maddy to trusted friends in Spain and diagnosed glandular fever as an explanation for her chronic morning sickness. Her depression was very real.

'Oh my God!' said Zara, a look of complete disbelief on her face. Lisa stared straight ahead, her face devoid of any expression.

'Also, around this time, one of Maddy's close friends committed suicide.'

'Patrick,' murmured Maddy. 'My poor, gentle Patrick.'

Archibold scanned the room for confirmation; a number of faces looked back at him. Nathan gave a short nod, and the lawyer continued. 'Using this tragedy as an excuse, Jon arranged with Maddy's school for a leave of absence on both psychological and personal grounds. He assured the school that Maddy would return to the UK fluent in Spanish, and with her completed coursework. Her pregnancy and the subsequent birth were therefore kept a secret, and her time away from school put down to a "temporary breakdown".'

Maddy squirmed within Zara.

'For reasons that Jon felt best at the time, Maddy was told she had given birth to a boy, and that the baby had died during the delivery. In reality, the baby was then passed over to contacts of Nathan's where it was temporarily fostered.'

Maddy remembered that day, the white, clinical space with the Spanish midwife, Nathan's voice in the delivery room, the news that her son had died and then the sorrow and emptiness that followed. She had blamed herself for his death, sure that God had punished her for what had happened. She could still recall the smell of the flowers on her bedside table, lilies – like the ones today in the churchyard. She'd hoped she'd never smell the scent of lilies again.

Zara shook her head in disbelief. 'Why tell her that her baby was dead?'

Nathan looked at Zara's tear-filled eyes. 'The pregnancy was not free of risk, Zara,' he told her. 'Maddy was very young and her body quite immature. It was a difficult birth and I was surprised the baby even survived. Maddy had been ill, physically and emotionally during the pregnancy, so we agreed that the removal of the baby, should it survive, would be the best option for her,' Nathan explained, yet again supporting Jon's version of events. But for him, it was another half-truth among so many lies. 'By telling Maddy that her baby had died, we hoped that she'd grieve and then move on. She was very young and had her whole life ahead of her.'

As the family took in the enormity of Jon's claims, Nathan's anguish for the part he'd played in Jon's plot intensified. He remembered how Maddy had taken the news of her baby's death. How pragmatic she had been, how her pale face had looked up into his and the sad weary smile she'd given him. 'Perhaps it's for the best,' she had said, turning away to face a blank wall. She never asked to see the baby. She never suspected that what he told her was a lie.

'So what really happened to Maddy's son?" asked Zara.

Four heads looked around to see who would answer. It was Jon's lawyer who spoke next.

'*The baby* was given to foster parents in Spain initially, then brought back to England.'

Lisa gave a loud cry as she reached for Zara's hand.

Zara sat silently, the information trickling through. 'I don't understand,' she said, looking at her mother. 'Where's Maddy's baby now?'

There was silence as the question hung ominously in the room.

'Upstairs!' Lisa sobbed, snatching her hand away from Zara and reaching for a tissue. '*She's* upstairs.'

Zara stood up, confusion written all over her face. 'Are you telling us that Maddy gave birth to a baby girl, not a boy? And the baby in question is … Pippa?'

The lawyers shuffled uncomfortably, each waiting for someone else to answer. Nathan turned towards Zara and smiled kindly. 'Yes, Zara,' he replied, looking directly into her anguished face. Pippa *is* Maddy's biological daughter.'

Zara went limp at the knees and dropped down onto the settee between her mother and Gareth.

Lisa tugged at her unyielding arm. 'I didn't know,' she whined. 'When Jon asked if we wanted to adopt a little girl, I had no idea it was Maddy's child.'

Zara turned and stared at her mother, her emotions raw and confused. 'If you'd known she was really Maddy's daughter, would you have said yes?'

'I don't know,' Lisa whispered, twisting in her seat, looking to her husband for answers.

Zara looked across at Jon in disgust. 'How could you do that to Maddy?' she asked.

'She didn't know. I didn't know,' howled Lisa in defence.

'So when did you find out, Mum?' asked Zara, her face now flushed with anger.

Lisa sobbed into her open hands. Lifting her face, she sniffed loudly. 'Today. I've just found out, Zara. Jon and Nathan told me earlier today. That's why they opened your note in Majorca – to check whether Maddy had made any reference to the baby.'

Zara swung round to face Jon. 'How could you do this?' she asked.

Jon, always in control, remained indifferent to the emotional outbursts from both Zara and Lisa; he'd been prepared for their reactions. Nothing came as a surprise to him, ever. All he had to do was play his part of the grieving and loving father well. Nathan, however, witnessed the women's meltdowns with both shame and discomfort.

Jon used his best professional voice: 'I'm sorry', he began, 'for how this all looks to you now, but I did what I did, regarding Pippa, for good reason.' He paused, his eyes quickly glancing from Lisa's face to Zara's. He knew he had their attention. 'My decision to convince Maddy that she had lost her baby was made to give my daughter a chance in life, without the handicap of being a young teenage mother. My choice to protect her may seem wrong to you now, but she was a minor and it was my decision and mine alone to make.' Jon sensed a shift in the women's demeanours as he looked over at them. Softening his voice, he continued, 'Never did I intend to give Maddy's baby away. I thought that by taking on the responsibility of the baby myself, I was helping Maddy, giving her a life outside of motherhood, not harming her. It was never my intent to hurt either Maddy or Pippa. Nor would I ever deliberately cause emotional distress to Lisa.'

Lisa lifted her chin and looked in Jon's direction, her eyes filled with hurt and confusion. Jon moved purposefully towards his wife, calmly taking her hand in his and raising it to his lips before continuing. 'Lisa wanted another child so badly. Pippa fulfilled her needs, and in taking Pippa into our home as our adopted daughter, I thought I'd made the best out of a tragic situation.'

Both legal parties watched Jon closely as he spoke, noting the change in Lisa's body language as she stroked his hand. The lawyers felt Jon's performance was outstanding, whether they believed he was morally right or not. *Bravo!* thought Michael, wanting to clap. *Masterful,* mouthed Archibold, moving towards Jon and patting him on the back in sympathy.

Potential crisis averted, Jon turned back towards his captive audience. 'Pippa was my blood and I wanted her back in the family,' he added. 'I'm sorry.'

There was a stunned silence, then a sob from Lisa.

Zara looked first at her distressed mother, then her step-father incredulously. 'But you lied to Maddy. You took her baby and told her it had died.'

'Shush ...' whispered Lisa, looking awkwardly at her daughter.

'I've explained why,' was Jon's clipped retort.

'So then you *adopted* the child, naming her Pippa,' Zara repeated, her mind processing the information again, her face flushed with barely controlled rage.

'Pippa needed a family, Zara,' said Lisa. 'And Jon was *protecting* Maddy.'

'How? By taking her child and pretending it was someone else's?' Zara uttered scornfully.

But I found out, Zara. The power of a mother's love, the connection that's never broken. Even now, Zara.'

Michael coughed delicately. 'I'm afraid there never was any *legal adoption* of Pippa.'

The air appeared to leave the room at Somes's revelation. Zara watched her mother collapse like a spent balloon.

As the news that there was no legal adoption fell over the assembled company, Nathan allowed his mind to drift back to his meeting with Maddy in Majorca, just prior to her death, when she'd confronted him about Pippa. The lies Nathan had lived with for so long weighed heavily. By admitting the truth to Maddy, as he did, he'd hoped there would be a chance for some peace at last. He had advanced cancer – a just punishment, he believed, each time he swallowed another painkiller. But now, his time was running out, and with Maddy's tragic death, his chance for absolution had been snatched away from him. Jon didn't know how close he had come to losing everything, how one of his faithful foot soldiers had finally betrayed his trust. But now Maddy would be buried with the truth, her truth: and he would surely die with his.

'The DNA says it all, doesn't it, Nathan?' Maddy had said to him, her expression so filled with hope, her tearful eyes brimming with questions. He'd never forgotten her pale, frightened face watching him from the maternity hospital bed; how she'd trusted him and he'd let her down. He'd tried to help in his own clumsy way after the baby was delivered, but Jon saw to that too. He didn't need to see the DNA proof regarding Pippa; he already knew the answer. She *was* Maddy's daughter. He'd been there at her birth; he was the one responsible for taking her away. And he was the one who gave her back to Jon, despite his own misgivings.

Maddy had left him that night in Majorca, standing alone, his head bowed as she walked away. 'Shame on you,' she had said. The last words he would ever hear from her. Now Jon was back in control. And he, Nathan, was still dancing to the puppeteer's pull, still cleaning up the mess, still pretending, still violating his Hippocratic Oath. A stab of pain brought him back to the present. Reaching into his pocket, he touched his pill bottle. Relief was at hand, but perhaps he needed the pain to help him function today. He knew there was more pain to come.

Chapter 15

L isa gulped back the tears as she looked askance at her husband. 'No adoption?' she eventually spluttered.

'There was no need,' said Jon, shrugging his shoulders. 'She was Maddy's daughter. I have the original birth certificate. As I said, it was always my decision to bring Pippa back home.'

'So why didn't you tell Mum the truth about her?' Zara asked.

Lisa continued to look at Jon, her bloodshot eyes brimming with tears.

'It could have been an awkward *ask*; we were getting married – your mother may have said no had she known Pippa was Maddy's daughter. I wasn't prepared to take that risk.'

'But what about Maddy's emotions during that time? She'd just lost her own baby and you were bringing one into her home.'

'I was devastated, Zara,' said Maddy, remembering that empty emotional hole that lay within her for years.

'Being so young,' Jon began, 'Maddy would have recovered from her baby's death quickly; she also believed her baby was a boy. The introduction of Pippa into the family at the time would have been beneficial for Maddy's state of mind.'

Jon's words sent shivers down Zara's spine.

'She was my salvation, Zara,' Maddy whimpered.

Zara shook her head in disbelief. 'It's all so wrong,' she moaned, sensing Maddy's pain. 'What you did would surely have broken Maddy's heart: her own father lying to her like that, taking away her baby. Anyone would *want* to die, learning their father was capable of such cruelty.'

Lisa wrapped her arms around Zara, the two of them sobbing. 'I'm so sorry, Zara. I wish I'd known at the beginning. Things might have worked out differently.'

Zara pulled back, staring at her mother. 'How different? Would you have given Pippa back to Maddy, Mum?' she asked.

Lisa's eyes frantically searched Jon's. 'I loved her as my own daughter,' she whispered.

'And I loved her as my own,' murmured Maddy.

Nodding her head, Zara smiled sadly. 'So that's a no. What a mess. But *who* then was Pippa's father?'

Nathan shuffled uncomfortably as he looked to Jon to provide the answer.

'I have my suspicions,' said Jon, 'but Maddy never told a soul. We must respect that; there is no need to know now. Pippa is safe within her rightful family. We don't need to complicate matters.'

'It's in the DNA, Zara,' said Maddy.

'So when will you tell Pippa that Maddy was her real mother?' asked Zara.

Lisa flinched, and Jon's eyes narrowed at the suggestion. 'We won't,' he said. 'I don't want Pippa to find out her mother was emotionally unstable and committed suicide.'

'Liar!' shrieked Maddy, desperate to get Zara's attention.

So angered by Jon's comments, Zara fought hard to control the sudden surge of emotions that made her want to hit out physically at him. Breathing in slowly and deeply, she willed her thumping heart to calm. She needed to stay in control.

'Breathe, Zara. Deep breaths. You must listen and stay calm. I need you to take all this in. There's more to come,' warned Maddy.

Hands clasped and fingers entwined, Michael nodded his grey-haired head. He'd been watching the exchange between the family from his seat by the fireplace. Wanting to be present, yet inconspicuous, he'd chosen to perch on the low antique milking stool, where his tall frame balanced precariously, his long legs folded like a crouching grasshopper. On cue, he slowly drew himself up from his seated position, his immaculately creased trousers falling perfectly back into shape as he unfolded himself to full height. Over six foot three inches tall, Michael struck a commanding pose, dressed in a pinstriped Savile Row jacket and trousers – or what he normally referred to as his 'battle suit'. Lifting his chin, he smiled to himself, his dark brown eyes beneath a pair of thick black eyebrows sparkling for a moment in Zara's direction. He disliked Jon Stone, he felt sorry for Lisa, but he admired Zara's strong performance. Maddy had been right about her decision to appoint her as Pippa's guardian.

'Would it be a good time now to continue with Maddy's will and wishes?' he volunteered. Removing his glasses, he faced the group, twiddling the delicate, metal-framed spectacles between the thumb and forefinger of his right hand. Archibold, short, thickset and uncomfortably squeezed into an ill-fitting suit, rubbed his hand over his well-oiled, shaven head. He found Michael's elegant stance and confident manner infuriating and looked aggressively towards him.

The group had now split into three camps: Jon with his lawyer, Archibold, and Lisa on the periphery, Nathan alone by the window and feisty Zara with Gareth. All faces turned towards Michael.

'May I remind you we are all here to hear Maddy's final wishes. I know all of us are saddened by her sudden departure and shocked by the latest revelation,' began Michael, before pausing and walking slowly towards the window where Nathan stood, then turning back to retrace his steps, twisting his glasses in his hand.

'Maddy came to visit me some months back with a story about a pregnancy and a birth that I admit I found difficult to comprehend.'

Across the room, Jon shuffled uncomfortably and Nathan lowered his head in embarrassment.

'As her lawyer, I explained I needed proof – birth certificates or even DNA to verify her claims.'

Jon's eyes flickered towards Nathan.

'I have in my possession results from samples of Pippa's and Maddy's DNA.' He paused a moment for reaction. 'These fully support her legal claim to be Pippa's biological and rightful mother.'

Zara twisted in her seat to confront the others. 'There! I told you. Maddy would never have committed suicide. She had too much to live for. She knew at the time of her death that Pippa was her daughter.'

'So it *was* just a dreadful accident,' said Gareth with some relief. The latest revelations had unsettled him greatly.

Michael looked sympathetically towards Zara. 'The circumstances of Maddy's demise may never be fully understood. However, back to Maddy's wishes for her daughter, Pippa.'

'Listen carefully, Zara, watch the reactions; you need to be on guard for Pippa's sake.'

Lisa pulled away from her husband, blowing her nose into a tissue. Jon's flinty eyes watched the concentration on Michael's face as he walked towards a small table where his briefcase lay to retrieve a number of documents.

Gareth and Zara both glanced around the room and then back at one another, their faces alive with questions. *What more are we about to discover?* thought Zara. She clasped Gareth's hand, and he squeezed hers back, reassuringly.

Lisa sat now slumped beside her daughter, her face pale and strained, her eyes closed, as if hoping she could shut out the inevitable.

Michael collated his paperwork and, with his glasses now perched on his nose, he continued, 'I'll now read out Madeline Stone's last will and testament.'

Zara saw the look of pure hatred that blazed for a second over Jon's carefully controlled features, and she shivered. Michael, seemingly oblivious to the effect he had created in the room, continued with the reading.

Zara found the legal jargon difficult to comprehend, but understood, in essence, that once Maddy reached the age of twenty-five she had an entitlement to the trust income from assets worth several millions. She had willed that her own personal funds and those she had received on her twenty-first birthday should be given to Pippa. In her will, she also asked that Zara should act as preferred legal guardian for Pippa and that she should manage her financial affairs until she reached the age of eighteen.

'Guardian?' interrupted Lisa, the panic rising in her voice. 'Why does Pippa need a guardian? She has Jon and me.'

Michael lifted his head from the paperwork and looked in Lisa's direction. Coughing politely, he continued, '… and that the jewellery, which had belonged to her mother and grandmother, and which had been given to Maddy on Tilly's death, should be secured by Zara and passed on to Pippa on her eighteenth birthday. Her boat, the *Phoenix*, is to be given to Pippa when she is able to command a vessel single-handed or reaches eighteen, whichever comes earliest. Until then, the trustees propose that it is to remain in the waters of Majorca—'

Lisa interrupted again at this point. 'I still don't understand the guardian issue. Are you saying Zara has rights over *us* with regard to Pippa's welfare? Pippa is *my* daughter and Jon's. Surely that's our decision?'

Michael looked at the visibly distraught Lisa and smiled kindly. He had expected this reaction; he expected more to come. 'Jon is Pippa's biological *grandfather*, Lisa. Maddy her *legal birth mother*! I'm sure Jon will not disagree with these facts,' he added, looking in Jon's direction. The returning scowl spoke volumes. 'But I'm sure Zara, as Maddy's preferred guardian, will allow Pippa to stay in an environment where she is safe and loved. As guardian she can oversee this. I can't see any difficulties here, can you, Zara?' he asked.

'You mean stay with Mum and Jon?' Zara looked at her mother's broken face. 'No,' she replied, hesitantly.

'Yes,' began Maddy, aware of all that was taking place around her. 'Be very careful, Zara.'

'So we can leave things as they are?' asked Lisa. 'Pippa believing Jon is her father and I'm her mother?'

Zara looked at Michael for approval, wondering again why Maddy had requested that she should be Pippa's guardian. He nodded wisely. 'It is you, Zara, who will have the right to decide such matters. And I'm sure any decision you make will be the appropriate one and made for Pippa's *benefit*.'

'Thank you,' mumbled Lisa, twisting the large solitaire diamond around her finger, mentally questioning whether it may have come from the Erskine estate. Confident now that Zara would do as she and Jon wished, she breathed more easily. Pippa would stay with them; the guardian issue was just a precaution and an unnecessary measure.

Michael noticed the trace of a frown on Zara's forehead. 'Don't worry, Zara. There will be many things to discuss, in private, at a later date,' he reassured her before returning to his reading of the will.

'Now, where was I? Oh yes, regarding the remaining funds in the Erskine Trust, they will be retained by the trust and distributed when Pippa Stone is twenty-one and twenty-five years of age. The family home in Wimbledon and the villa in Majorca can only be inhabited by those responsible for maintaining Pippa's wellbeing and upbringing. Once she is twenty-five, both these properties will fully revert back to Pippa, to do with as she wishes according to the guidelines set out by the Erskine Trust.'

Lisa looked across at her husband, who chose that moment to look away, mentally adding up the years he would have left in their current homes should Pippa decide to take possession of her full inheritance at twenty-five.

There was complete silence as Zara searched the faces around the room. Today had been one of the worst she could have ever imagined. Firstly, burying Maddy, then the dramatic truth about Pippa and now the final, agonising surprise of Maddy's will and her wishes. She looked up at Michael, emotionally drained. 'Do you need anything further from me at this point?' she asked.

Taking in Zara's strained features, he shook his head. 'No, I'm done here. I can talk to you another time,' he answered.

Relieved, Zara stood. 'Then if you'll all excuse me, I need to take some time out. Today has been a tremendous strain on us all, and the latest news – well, it's *finished* me. If you don't mind, I'd like some space to think, in private.'

There was a subtle nodding of heads as she left, in search of refuge in her bedroom. What she'd just heard made her stomach turn. When Gareth found her some time later, he looked as sick as she felt.

'Has Michael gone?' she asked.

'Yes. He said he'll call you over the next few days and set up an appointment to discuss things further.'

'How's Maddy's will going down out there?' she asked, knowing full well what the answer would be.

Gareth's white strained face betrayed his anxiety. 'Not good. Nathan's trying his best to calm the situation, but Jon's suggesting taking legal action against Maddy's wishes.'

'Can he?' asked Zara.

'Don't know. Archie says he'll look into it.'

'That man's an oaf,' replied Zara. 'Maddy never liked him, couldn't bear him in the house either – used to tell me to make sure Pippa and I were somewhere else if he called in.'

'I get the impression he and Jon go back a long way and Nathan seems to be connected in some way too. There's been a lot of hidden messages in the looks they've all been giving one another – didn't you notice?'

Zara shook her head. 'I've been too shocked to notice anything.'

'Well, Jon's now in a foul mood and drinking Scotch. He's furious Maddy made you Pippa's legal guardian.'

'Oh, God,' whispered Zara, her head heavy in her hands. 'What has Maddy left me?'

'Pippa's not safe, Zara,' whispered Maddy. 'You mustn't let my father take control. Speak to Michael.'

'She's left you a mess, Zara,' stated Gareth, pacing the room in distress. 'A bloody mess.'

Zara nodded in submission. 'I still don't fully understand what the legal implications are for me in all this. I need to speak to Michael; I've got so many questions. Maddy made me Pippa's legal guardian for a reason and I must respect that and try and understand why. I also need to do what's best for everyone, including my poor mother.' Zara turned her head, searching Gareth's eyes. 'How was she after I left?'

Gareth lowered himself down onto the bed, stretching out beside Zara. 'She's in pieces. Her whole world has collapsed around her, and right now, Jon is being far from supportive. He's angry with Michael and, ultimately, Maddy.'

Zara shuddered. 'I wonder at what point Maddy realised Pippa was her own daughter? She may have even have thought Mum knew too.'

Gareth shook his head sadly. 'I don't understand how she managed to keep everything secret for so long. It's all such a sorry sad mess … and poor little Pippa hasn't begun to understand what's been happening around her.'

Zara sighed deeply. 'She mustn't be told anything yet. Not until we've fully understood the legalities and how best to handle the whole mess.'

Gareth nodded in agreement.

'I was hard on Mum, wasn't I?' Zara asked, looking to the one remaining person she trusted.

Gareth's face remained blank as he tried to make sense of the revelations. 'It's not your mum's fault, Zara. She was duped too.'

Zara turned towards him. 'I realise that now. The trouble is, love can sometimes make you too forgiving, or even blind to what's really bad or wrong.'

'And don't I know it,' whispered Maddy.

A sudden thought crossed Gareth's mind. 'What happens to your mother if Jon decides to leave her?' he asked, sitting bolt upright.

Zara looked at Gareth with alarm. 'She sold her home. God knows where the money went, so I guess she'd be homeless; she couldn't claim half of Jon's house – it's not even his!' As the enormity of the facts became clear, Zara shuddered. 'What's more, as Pippa was never legally adopted by Mum or Jon, she has no rights or access to her daughter.'

'*You mean* my *daughter, Zara,*' hissed Maddy.

Gareth's brows knitted as he grimaced. 'There's something else that's been troubling me.'

'What?' asked Zara, twisting onto her elbow, her heart pounding in her chest.

'Why this elaborate scheme to persuade your mother to adopt an unknown child? Doesn't make sense unless …'

'Unless what?' asked Zara, her stomach now in sickening knots.

Gareth shook his head, struggling with what he was about to say. 'Do you think it's possible Jon picked and married your mum purely to provide a mother for Maddy's child? He'd obviously decided to keep her well in advance.'

Zara's hand flew to her lips. Her mouth tasted bitter and her eyes flickered as she thought back to their whirlwind romance. It had all happened so fast. They'd apparently met on an internet dinner dating site, and after one meal together, Lisa had convinced herself that Jon was the one. Desperate to start her own life with Gareth, Zara had happily encouraged her mother to take things further and not to hang around. Jon appeared to be a good catch – in his late forties, and a well-respected professional consultant psychiatrist living in a beautiful home in Wimbledon, with housekeepers and a villa abroad. What was there not to like about such a man? So, encouraged by her daughter, Lisa had let her guard down and Jon had swiftly swept her off her feet.

'Did your mother ever talk about wanting another child?' Gareth asked, cutting into Zara's thoughts. She shook her head. 'No. She never mentioned wanting another baby. At least, not until Jon came onto the scene.'

'Didn't you think it strange, at her age?'

Zara looked at Gareth. 'Perhaps I did, but Mum seemed so keen.'

'But the idea definitely came *after* Jon appeared on the scene?'

'Yes.'

'And not before?'

'Well, no. She wasn't in a position to have another child, even if she'd wanted one.'

Gareth got off the bed, taking a few paces around the bedroom. There were too many factors that didn't add up; if Jon had already made up his mind about keeping Maddy's baby, all he would need was a willing partner, a new wife who he could persuade to adopt her. He stopped looking directly at Zara. What she saw mirrored her own thoughts.

'He stole my baby, Zara.'

'How long did they "try" themselves before Pippa arrived? It wasn't long, was it?'

Zara listened, shaking her head.

'Still doesn't add up, Zara. Why the elaborate scheme to hide the truth from everyone and dupe your mother? Why not tell the truth?'

'Jon said protection for Maddy. She was too young to be a mother.'

'Granted, but why not tell his new wife the truth?' Gareth thought back to a party he'd attended at the Wimbledon property when Maddy was fourteen. One of his friends, Tom, had a sister at the same school as Maddy, and the two boys, Gareth and Tom, although older, had been invited to make up the numbers. It had been an awkward affair, a few boys he didn't know, and the girls all too young to be of interest to either Tom or Gareth. Realising now that Maddy must have been pregnant around that period shocked Gareth. 'I'm still finding Maddy's secret pregnancy too unbelievable to comprehend.'

'Why?'

'Because she didn't look like … that sort of girl.'

'Meaning what?'

'Well, she was so … little; even dressed up she looked little. Not womanly.'

'You mean she didn't have huge breasts and curvaceous hips?'

Gareth grinned. 'You know what I mean. We boys looked for the mature, adventurous girls – the ones that flirted openly.'

'And Maddy didn't look like that or flirt?'

'No.'

'Well, she must have done something more than *flirting*, Gareth. She got pregnant by someone she knew back then. Who were her friends at the time?'

Gareth shrugged. 'Didn't know many of them. I remember Chloe, her best friend. I met her once at a Wimbledon party. Her brother was there too – Patrick, the one who killed himself. After that, we never met up again and Maddy went away.'

'Do you think Patrick could have been the father?' asked Zara.

'Patrick? And that's why he killed himself?' Gareth remembered the slim, lanky youth with his effeminate features and blond, wavy hair. 'It's possible, I suppose. 'Would his sister, Chloe, know?' asked Zara.

'I don't know,' Gareth said, shaking his head. 'Chloe and her family left Wimbledon after Patrick died. Their name was Darcy. I'm sure we could track her down, but what for? If he was Pippa's father, he's not much use to her now.'

Zara sighed deeply. 'Poor Maddy. If that was the case, and he *was* the father, no wonder she needed antidepressants. What about the housekeeper at the time? Surely she'd have suspected something?' suggested Zara. 'Would she remember someone in particular who may have hung around with Maddy back then?'

'No, I don't think she'd be much help. I do remember her, skinny and hard-faced, smoked like a chimney. She never noticed a thing, even our illegal drinking binge with Jon in his den that night. And who knows if she's still alive. Perhaps we're just not supposed to find out, Zara.'

Zara's mind was in turmoil. 'Maybe. Well, whatever the real parentage issues are, Pippa will never want for love or security as she grows older.'

'Providing you watch over her,' said Maddy.

Chapter 16

It was five fifteen in the morning when Zara woke. She'd forgotten to bring a glass of water to bed and needed a drink. Quietly, she slipped out of Gareth's arms and padded towards the bathroom. She filled a toothbrush glass with some bottled water, sipping slowly to clear her muddled head.

'Oh, Maddy,' she whimpered. 'I'm so sorry. I wish you could tell me what I'm supposed to do. There's so much hurt and anger around me, and I can't think straight. If you can hear me, help me. I'm sinking here ...'

Maddy was only too aware of Zara's confusion. She could sense the anguish and fear that pumped through her body. She needed Zara to understand the whole story before it was too late. She'd been allowed to stay for a purpose and she had no idea how much longer she would be given. 'Zara,' she prompted.

Zara was sitting on the toilet now, her head resting in her hands. Lifting her face, she listened.

'Zara ... can you hear me?'

'Maddy? Is that you?' she whispered, incredulous, her eyes darting nervously around the room.

'Yes, it's me. I need your help.'

Zara rubbed her eyes and shook her head. Disorientated and confused, she doubted what she was hearing, but Maddy's voice seemed so clear in her head.

'Go to the mirror.'

Zara got up and stood in front of the bathroom mirror, seeing only her own pale face and sleep-glued hair.

'Look with your heart, Zara, not your eyes. Close your eyes and feel my love for you.'

As Zara closed her eyes, she felt her heart burst open in response and a sense of pure happiness rushed through her. Opening her eyes once more, she looked into the mirror and there she saw Maddy looking back at her.

'Hello, Zara.'

Zara caught her breath as the image in front of her began to quiver.

'Please don't be frightened,' Maddy begged. 'I don't understand how this works either, but I need you to work with me.'

Zara stared at the mirror. She didn't feel frightened, just distrustful of what she was seeing. 'I think I could be going mad,' she whispered to the reflection, rubbing the glass with her hand. 'Tell me you aren't really doing this.'

'I am. And you can't rub me away, Zara. I'm appearing from within you.'

Zara gently prodded her own face, watching the indentation appear on Maddy's in the mirror. Then, snatching her hand away, she stepped back and shivered.

'Damn!' muttered Maddy. 'Why does that keep on happening, just as I think I've got through to her?'

Zara warily observed her own reflection at a distance. 'Maddy, I don't know if you can hear me, but, I know about Pippa being your daughter. We all do … now. I also know how you ensured your grandmother's inheritance was secured and invested for Pippa; and I've agreed to be her legal guardian. You can rest easy now. I'll see that all's done as you would want. There's no need to worry.'

'Oh, but I do, Zara … I worry very much. You have no idea of the dangers on your own doorstep.' But no matter how Maddy tried, the connection between herself and Zara had dropped.

'Zara, is that you?' Gareth's voice called out. 'Who are you talking to?'

Zara looked one more time at the image in the mirror: the tousled dark curls, the round face with wide cheekbones housing a pair of sad brown eyes. 'No one,' she called out, 'just me,' she whispered, moving towards the bathroom door.

'Come back to bed,' Gareth told her.

'I am.'

'Look for the answers ... the secret beach, Zara,' Maddy pleaded.

Zara climbed back into bed and attempted to sleep, tossing and turning, her restless dreams punctuated by images of a small, deserted, inlet beach.

⟨⟩

Later that morning, Zara rang Michael, making an appointment to visit him.

'Happier now?' asked Gareth.

'Yes, I still have some questions, and I need to ensure that whatever Maddy wanted done is done as *she* wanted. That's all I can do for her now.'

'Be prepared, Zara. There's a lot more at stake than you realise.'

Chapter 17

With the expensive legal cogs still turning and Maddy now buried, Jon's intention was to return to the Pink Villa in Majorca, taking Lisa and Pippa with him to enjoy the end of the late summer. Lisa had been reluctant to revisit, mumbling about Maddy's possible ghostly presence, but Jon had bluntly dismissed her ideas as ludicrous, suggesting she went ahead, taking both Zara and Gareth with her. As the young couple's engagement celebrations had been cut short, they both agreed. They planned to visit the Old Town in Ibiza and reclaim some of their 'engagement' happiness.

When Zara told Michael of her plans, he told her about a friend of Maddy's who also lived in Ibiza. A month before her accident, Maddy had sent Michael an envelope containing special instructions. In this, she had requested that another party be looked after, should something happen to her. It was this individual's name that he passed over to Zara now, advising her that there was something of Maddy's left there that needed to be collected. He didn't know what it was, making it all the more intriguing for Zara, who kept this little piece of information to herself, preferring not to encourage speculation or unwanted interest.

During a number of meetings with Michael in his Dorking offices, Zara had discussed the complications and implications surrounding the Erskine Trust. She'd been shocked and surprised to learn just how meticulous Maddy had been in protecting her grandmother's inheritance. Zara, like Michael, found Maddy's attention to detail uncomfortable in someone so young; it was as if she'd expected to die. According to Michael, by the age of eighteen, Maddy had given him full and objective instructions in the event of her own untimely death. By twenty-one, these had changed again. During her last visit, she came with astonishing news and new instructions. It was then that she provided him with the name and proof of the next Erskine heir: Pippa.

Now, armed with the address in Ibiza, Zara had every intention of visiting this mystery person and beneficiary in Maddy's will.

On the morning of their arrival back at the Pink Villa, Lisa was greeted warmly by Emily and Pedro. Wiry and fit, Pedro carried out most of the lighter gardening; his youngest son, Peppi, was the main groundsman. Between them, the Majorcan-born family ran and maintained the villa. Emily was small and thickset, with dark, sun-weathered skin and deep brown eyes. It was difficult to estimate Emily's and Pedro's ages because of their boundless energy, but the thick grey weaves in their dark, curly hair and deeply etched creases around their eyes suggested a long life. Emily's girth was thicker than her husband's, a result of many pregnancies being her excuse, but Pedro affectionately blamed it on her cooking. Born and raised a Catholic, after the death of her one and only female baby, Emily had turned towards a mix of religions, old and new, favouring some unconventional views and spiritual leanings to help her understand 'her God's' plans.

That evening, after dinner, Emily watched how Pippa moved cautiously around the patio area, keeping close to Lisa or Zara, her eyes darting towards the shadowed areas of the garden. Smiling, Emily walked towards them. She carried a bowl filled with offerings: sea salt, fresh rosemary, sage sprigs, lavender leaves and heads, fresh basil and juniper berries. 'For us, to throw tonight,' she told them. 'It's time for the little one to let Maddy go; no more fear, just love.' Then, looking at Pippa, she added, 'Come. Come with me, I'll take you to where she fell. There are no ghosts, my sweet one. Just her love.'

Pippa, glancing over at Zara, placed her hand into Emily's outstretched palm.

'Will you come too, Zara?' Emily asked.

Zara looked into Emily's kind, sparkling eyes and nodded, beckoning to her mother. Perhaps this Majorcan woman could lay to rest the ghosts of that dreadful day. It was worth a try.

'We're all going to visit the place where Maddy fell,' Zara whispered to Gareth out of Pippa's earshot. 'Emily wants us to let Maddy go.'

'Surely you two don't believe in all that stuff?' asked Gareth in alarm, watching Lisa place her arm around Zara's shoulder.

Lisa smiled. 'Yes, actually I do. I know Emily can sense and see things we can't, so I'll happily go with her and say goodbye to Maddy.'

'Well, as long as you don't make the spot where she fell into a shrine. Jon won't be happy if you do anything like that,' added Gareth, feeling uncomfortable with the talk of ghosts, and more uncomfortable still when he saw them walking away, realising he was now left alone.

'Hold on. I might come with you,' he called out, quickly following them.

The sun was dropping over the sparkling sea as the group made their way to the stone balustrade. Standing here, they could see down part of the pathway and out to the stretch of sea.

'Ah, so beautiful out there on the ocean. No wonder Maddy wanted to sail around this island forever,' said Zara.

'And I hope she's at peace now and has forgiven her father's misguided and clumsy attempts at making things good,' said Lisa, in an obvious reference to Jon's decisions regarding Pippa. It wasn't an endorsement of what he'd done, but neither was it a rebuff. The family were still split on the rights and wrongs of Pippa's so-called 'adoption'. Zara felt Jon's actions unjustifiable and wrong; Gareth too. But Lisa, having *gained* by what happened, wavered from her sense of misplaced pity and that of her own happiness. The uncomfortable truth that Maddy was Pippa's *real* mother would remain a well-kept family secret, only to be spoken about in closed circles, if at all.

On the walk down the pathway, Pippa held Lisa's hand tightly. Emily had been right in pushing the group to carry out this exercise. Without closure, the walk down to the beach would have become a nightmare for the more sensitive among them. With the police tapes gone, there was nothing to suggest that an accident had taken place here.

Emily stood in the centre of the path as she murmured words in Mallorquí. They seemed to be part chant, part prayer, part new-age spiritual – the words meant nothing to the assembled group, but the sentiments were understood. Emily was helping them to say goodbye to Maddy, for good, and as she sprinkled the herbs and salt around the path, then threw a small handful over the edge and finally into the soft breeze, she mumbled a final private prayer. When the pot was empty she lifted her face to the group. 'Gone! All gone … only her love remains.'

'That's true,' thought Maddy, watching the exorcism display with amusement. 'You can't wipe away my love. Ever. But poor Emily, if only you realised I'm unable to "go" anywhere just yet.'

Before retiring to bed that night, Lisa quietly asked Gareth and Zara if they thought Patrick Darcy could have been Pippa's father. Zara looked at Gareth, who raised his shoulders in a shrug.

'We don't know, Mum,' Zara replied. 'But it's a possibility.'

'Perhaps that's why he killed himself. And that's why Maddy never spoke of him to anyone,' ventured Lisa, twisting the stem of her wine glass between her thumb and forefinger. 'Poor girl. Do you think we could find out? DNA or whatever? Done discreetly, obviously,' she suggested. 'I don't want Jon to know anything about this conversation. For some reason, he doesn't like to be reminded of Patrick, which makes me wonder if I'm right. And if I am, poor Pippa will have lost both her parents through suicide—'

Surprised by her mother's suggestion, Zara interrupted. 'Mum, I don't think Pippa's DNA will tell us very much more. We have nothing to compare it to.'

'Oh, but it will tell you lots,' murmured Maddy, watching the exchange through Zara's eyes.

Zara looked towards Gareth for his input.

'Perhaps Nathan might be able to help,' he suggested, aware of an undercurrent of unease in Lisa's request.

'Ok, I'll ask him, if you like?' replied Zara, now worried by the strange, vacant look on her mother's face. 'Ok, Mum?'

Lisa snapped her head back and focused on her daughter. 'Please, but discreetly.'

Chapter 18

Clutching the address Michael had given her, Zara climbed the steep steps of the Old Town of Ibiza, until she found the shop, tucked in between an antique jeweller's and a boutique selling hand-painted silk and tie-dyed cotton clothing. The shop's sign read *the secret beach*, and the narrow entrance led to a rickety wooden staircase that dropped down into a large basement, with whitewashed walls on which hung the most exquisite paintings Zara had ever seen. Picking her feet across the hessian carpet, she stopped at one, sucking in her breath as she shed tears of joy. A large watercolour, it depicted a beautiful young woman dressed in a flowing cream garment, walking among the gentle surf. In her outstretched arms she carried the moon, a full translucent globe from which the haunting face of a young child looked out. It wasn't so much the overall image that moved Zara, but the actual faces in it. As she looked at the young woman, she could almost hear her whispering back to her.

'I call that one *Hidden Child*,' a voice said.

Zara turned slowly, aware of the tears rolling down her cheeks.

'It moves me too ... every time I look at the love on the mother's face,' the owner of the voice continued with a gentle smile.

Zara watched her beautiful long fingers flutter in the air as she spoke. 'It's one of my favourites, very precious to me,' she whispered, her hands now clasped as if in prayer and pulled towards her breast. 'The power of a mother's love,' she murmured. 'She finally found her lost child.'

The woman paused, looking into Zara's eyes, registering the tears and the pale face. 'Zara?' She tilted her face on one side. 'Are you Zara?'

Zara nodded, a lump somewhere within her throat making her mute.

'Michael said you were coming, and you look just like Maddy described. I'm so sorry, Zara. I haven't introduced myself properly. I'm Izzy, a good friend of Maddy's.' Izzy extended her hand and Zara shook it. 'I didn't expect you today. I should have spoken to you ... before you saw the paintings.'

Zara, her brown eyes sparkling, placed a hand on Izzy's arm. 'It's fine. I should have called you first. They're quite beautiful, so hauntingly real, just took me by surprise. Did you paint them?'

'Yes,' Izzy answered as Zara moved on towards the next, a seascape at sunset, painted in greens and blues with the gold and orange of the burning sun reflecting off the dark water. Above the sky, caught in the dying sun's rays, Zara could make out the outstretched wings of a fiery angel, its face – Maddy's – looking down on the churning sea.

'Oh my God. This is so incredible—' Zara broke off, her tears falling freely now. 'You've caught her perfectly; she looks as if she's part of the sunset, part of the air ...'

Standing next to Zara, Izzy nodded, smiling lovingly at the composition. 'That one is new. I painted it for Pippa; I wanted her to see her mother in all her glory, looking down from up high across the sea. I wanted her to feel her love, to know that wherever she may go in the world, she will always be watched over.'

'You knew Pippa?' Zara asked, amazed that this woman appeared to know so much about her sister, yet she'd only just found out about Izzy from Michael.

'Yes, Maddy introduced me to Pippa. She spoke about you too, all the time,' said Izzy.

Zara found herself close to breaking, looking back at the painting. 'Is that how you imagine her now? As an angel in the sky?' she asked.

Izzy paused. 'Yes ... my beautiful angel. All-powerful, all-seeing, forever strong, forever loved.' Izzy turned back towards Zara. 'You must forgive me, Zara. When I lost Maddy, I lost a part of me. Painting is my way of bringing her back. I'm sorry, you must find all this very strange, not least uncomfortable. But when I paint, I can talk to her.'

Maddy watched Izzy's eyes through Zara's, noting the dark smudges beneath them, the gauntness of her beautiful face and the new frailty in her slim body. 'If only you knew how close I am to you,' she whispered. 'If only you could speak directly to me, one last time.'

'Let me close up the shop, and then we can talk,' said Izzy. 'I know you must have many questions for me.'

Maddy watched Izzy climb the stairs, up to the shop's front door. She listened to the familiar drop of the catch and the sound of her dainty feet as they tripped down the wooden stairs again, towards Zara, and noticed her straightening her beige silk shift dress and smiling. Maddy felt her heart leap.

A powerful sense of emotion flooded through Zara. Hunting for tissues, she dragged the half-open pack out of her overcrowded bag, watching as shreds of used tissues fluttered onto the carpet. 'Sorry,' she mumbled, dropping onto one knee to pick them up.

'Please, Zara. Don't worry. Here, come sit with me.'

Zara followed Izzy's outstretched arm to the white leather settee set against the back wall. She watched her elegant body fold as she sat down, patting the cushion next to her. 'You must be so confused!'

'I am,' replied Zara. 'It's all so horrible and sad. I still can't get my head around it all.'

'And now you've found me.' Izzy chuckled softly. 'What did Michael tell you about me?'

'He told me very little, just that you were a secret beneficiary of Maddy's will and last wishes, and that you had something for me from her.'

Izzy nodded, looking deeply into Zara's eyes. 'Maddy told me a great deal about you, Zara; she described your lovely face perfectly, right down to those eyes of yours. "Pools of liquid treacle" was her description.'

Zara chuckled. 'You knew her well?'

Izzy smiled, a faint pull on her perfect rose mouth. 'I knew her … completely.'

Deep within Zara, Maddy ached with love. Here, so close, sat the very woman she had wanted to spend the rest of her life with. Her need to touch Izzy was so powerful.

Aware of the unexplained emotional shift within her body, Zara began to tremble.

Izzy placed one hand on hers to still her, then tilting her face back towards the second painting she smiled gently, the over-head light on the wall reflecting on her glossy dark hair. Beneath her lowered lashes Zara glimpsed a shimmering tear.

'You loved her!' Zara gasped, Maddy's choice of sexual partner suddenly apparent.

'Yes. I loved her, we loved one another, we were going away together, taking Pippa. It was all planned, but then—'

'Taking Pippa?'

'Of course. She was so close to getting the one thing she always wanted: her daughter. I was someone she fell in love with on her journey towards that goal.'

'I never even knew about Pippa being her own daughter, or you. I feel I never really knew Maddy at all.'

Izzy turned her face towards Zara, the glistening tear

slipping from her sea-green eyes. 'There was a great deal Maddy never told anyone.'

'How did you find out about her death? We didn't tell you because we didn't know of your existence. I'm so sorry.'

'Michael told me, although I knew something must have happened to her when she didn't return.'

'I'm so sorry, Izzy. If only we'd known …'

'How could you? Maddy kept our relationship secret.'

Zara shook her head in sadness. 'I wish she'd have told me'

Izzy smiled. 'Michael was very professional and very kind to me. It was obvious he cared a great deal for Maddy and was equally enraged by what she'd discovered.'

'So unbelievably wrong,' uttered Zara.

Izzy placed her hand over Zara's. 'I knew something was wrong before he contacted me. She never called me that day, and I couldn't get hold of her. I knew in my heart that something bad must have happened.'

Zara dropped her head, understanding what this woman must have felt and the pain she too had suffered.

'I visited the villa after the accident, when you were away in England. I saw the police accident tapes, I read the local news. It was like … a part of me had broken off, and I was in limbo, waiting for her. I knew how Maddy wanted me to make a success of *the secret beach*. She used to tell me talent needs finance. She was right. I can stay here now and paint, although my heart wants to break each time I walk down those stairs into this basement. We had such plans …' Izzy paused. 'I used to dance – ballet, that is. I was what they called a child prodigy. But I fell out of love with ballet school when I met my first boyfriend; our two worlds weren't compatible – he wanted risk, speed, motorbikes and skiing trips. I had curfews, strict diets and a "no-risk" ruling. But we were in love. Or so I thought. I was expelled from ballet school in the end for poor discipline and lack of dedication – that and the fact that we drove to Marseille on the back of his Harley that summer and I missed an enrolment date. The motorbikes won. It felt like something out of *West Side Story*, only my "Tony" didn't die, he just went off with someone else. Heartbroken, I turned to art, expressing my emotions on canvas and paper. I enrolled at art school, and from there I wound up in Ibiza on an artist retreat weekend and never went back. I used to paint to live, now I live to paint. Maddy made all that possible.

Zara took Izzy's hand in hers and squeezed it gently.

'Michael told me that Maddy had left instructions.' Izzy withdrew her hand and waved it at the surrounding walls. 'The gallery and the house above, where I paint, are mine now. Maddy bought them for me ... before she died. It was going to be my place of work, our first business venture, this and her boat. In time we would return to the Pink Villa, as her grand-mother wanted, and continue with our lives there and here.'

'And Pippa?' asked Zara.

'Ah, Pippa ... she would stay with us. Maddy wanted her schooled somewhere warm, near the water, close to her. She'd waited so long for her own daughter, the thought of sending her away to school was too much for her to bear.'

'How long did Maddy know Pippa was her daughter?'

Izzy's eyes glanced towards the painting of the mother with the moon in her hands. 'She told me she always felt something more than sisterly love for Pippa. She described her feelings as being like an umbilical cord that connected them both, an uncut cord made from pure love. As Pippa grew, the sense of connection strengthened for her. She kept her thoughts and emotions in check, never daring to believe completely, always looking for the proof she needed.'

'So what made her sure?'

'Old photos she found of her grandmother and mother as a child. The albums had been packed up years ago and obviously forgotten about. She found them one summer, in a box, in the roof space of the villa. She showed them to me. There was such a strong resemblance between Pippa and Maddy's own mother as a toddler. That and the tongue rolling.'

'Tongue rolling?'

Izzy chuckled. 'Yes, not everyone can roll their tongues. It's a characteristic that is passed down genetically. Just one of the small "nudges" that made her sure Pippa was hers.'

'Nudges?' asked Zara.

'Yes, that's what she referred to them as. Nudges, like Pippa's widow's peak, just like her own mother's, an index finger on Pippa's hand, the same shape as her own, and different to the rest of the digits. Little things that no one else would notice, except someone in love with her own child.'

'Oh my God. I remember the tongue-rolling games. So she believed that was a possible hereditary link?'

'Yes; only a possible one, but when added to all the others—'

'We used to laugh about how similar Pippa's mannerisms were to Maddy's; we used to blame it on Maddy spending too much time with her', said Zara with a smile.

'I know. That's what everyone thought.'

'So she went on to prove it with DNA?'

'Yes. Mouth swabs, hair follicles, hers and Pippa's. The results were positive. Pippa *was* her own daughter. Michael was as shocked as everyone else must have been.'

'I still can't believe it's true. It all sounds like a creepy Victorian gothic novel: daughter has child stolen from her and given to wicked stepmother. Only my mother isn't wicked, and she loved Pippa as her own. It's Jon that is to blame in all of this. Why couldn't he have just allowed Maddy to keep Pippa? It's not such a bad thing to have a baby with no father present in this day and age.'

'I think it was more than that. I think it was something to do with Maddy's age when she conceived. That alone would have raised some questions.'

'Ah, Jon's reputation as the perfect father?' mocked Zara.

Izzy sniffed, looking away in thought. 'Maddy had many secrets in her life. Like ours, a very special one; a life-changing one. She wanted to keep our true relationship a secret … for a bit longer.'

To hug it to myself, to remember how we fought it, how we never expected to feel as we did, *thought Maddy, her memories replaying those hesitant moments alone on the boat, the long, exquisite wait as they walked back to the gallery, the intensity of their mutual touching, the pure burst of real pleasure, with no fear, no pain and no regrets. Theirs had been a physical love Maddy had never experienced before; and would never feel again.*

'I wish she'd have shared some of this with me. If I'm honest, I feel … jealous, almost. All this time, all the secrets: you, Pippa and her plans to leave,' said Zara. 'And I knew nothing.'

'But she couldn't tell you, Zara … too much depended on secrecy. She even left her phone with me so any arrangements were made by me, on her instructions. "Nothing left to chance, or left behind," were her words.'

'We searched for her phone!' exclaimed Zara.

'I know,' said Izzy. 'Jon called the number constantly after her death. She left her phone with me deliberately. We communicated via a disposable mobile.'

Maddy remembered how she'd removed the sim card that night, after her meeting at the beach, watching as both the card and phone sank deep into the water beside the Phoenix.

'She never wanted Jon to get access to her phone; so much was stored on it for the future and her case. She also left something with me, for you, as you know.'

Izzy walked towards a painted cabinet, pulled out a phone and a book from a drawer and passed them both over to Zara. 'The phone is locked. Her password is the word "secret" – you need to enter the corresponding numerals. In her emails, you'll find copies of all the documentation and results required to support her claims ... and more, Zara.'

'And this? Her journal – have you read it?' Zara asked, placing the phone beside her as she opened the hardcover book Izzy gave her.

'She read it to me. We spoke about what happened to her in the past, and we were working through the pain of denial and fear. She'd come so far and still remained so amazingly forgiving. That's one thing Maddy did: forgive people. I guess that's how she survived all that happened to her.'

'Did she tell you who Pippa's father was?'

'Yes.'

'Who was he?'

Izzy closed her eyes briefly, then opened them again, smiling at Zara.

'You're not going to tell me, are you?'

Izzy shook her head.

'Did she write it in here?'

Izzy smiled. 'There's enough information for you to understand.'

Zara skimmed the familiar and well-loved writing. 'Was it Patrick?'

Izzy's eyes locked onto Zara's.

'Please, Izzy, who was it?' implored Zara.

'What she wants you to know ... is in the journal. She has

the DNA results to back it all up.' Izzy stretched out her hand, placing it on Zara's arm. 'You must understand, Maddy gave this to me for safekeeping. She didn't expect to die when she did. She didn't want Pippa's name to be sensationalised, or dragged through the courts. She wanted to handle it all with a sense of ... "forgiveness". She expected Jon to let her take Pippa away from him and start a new life. He knew she had the DNA to support her claims, and she didn't want revenge for what had happened to her; just Pippa, and what was hers legally, a second chance.'

Zara nodded. Flipping through the book, her eyes caught on the entry headed 'My childhood'. Scanning, she gasped at some of the content, her eyes wide and questioning. 'Am I understanding this correctly?' Zara asked, a look of shock on her face.

'Yes,' Izzy answered quietly, noting how pale Zara had suddenly become. 'Please, Zara, read this carefully. No gut reactions It's not what Maddy wanted.'

'Oh, but it is now, my beautiful Izzy. Gut reaction may be the only way. You have no idea of the lengths he's gone to in order to protect himself,' whispered Maddy, fully aware of the conversation taking place between her stepsister and her lover. 'There's more, much more ... and I need you both to find out the truth, before it's too late.'

'Then this means ...' Zara broke off, her mouth filled with bile, her stomach twisting with disgust.

'Yes, my sweet Zara ... that's what Maddy had to forgive.' *'And so much more ...'*

⁓

Watching Zara climb the stairs and leave the shop, Izzy felt a building sense of unease. She'd known instinctively when something had happened to Maddy. She'd felt it, like a sudden rip to her insides, a primeval sense of fear that started in her stomach and spread to her heart. Then came the coldness, a deep coldness, that bit deep. She'd prayed and cried. The phone was useless; she could do nothing but wait. After a while the connection she felt to Maddy just went dead, as if a light switch had been turned off. Izzy had grappled with her own emotions, a sense of panic and loss churning within her.

When she received that call from Michael, she already knew what he was about to tell her. Previously, for Izzy, the loss of a loved one had manifested with the reassuring sense of smell, a waft of perfume or hair shampoo, something the person had used while alive, or a vague shape just flickering out of the corner of her eyes and the welcoming feeling of warmth. With Maddy's death Izzy experienced none of these. Maddy had simply gone – and for both of them, that couldn't be right.

But just now, when Zara turned to say goodbye, Izzy saw something behind her eyes ... something that shouldn't have been there, and it frightened her. She needed to speak to her friend Mathew quickly. Only he would understand her fears.

Closing the door behind her, Izzy climbed up to the street. She knew what she was thinking was improbable, but in her heart she believed it. She'd seen the look behind Zara's eyes, touched the energy radiating through her skin, felt the love of her lover, all coming from within Zara. If she was right, as frightening as it sounded, Maddy was 'inside' her stepsister.

Making her way up to the top of the walled fortress, Izzy found Mathew, one of the town's mystic men. She sat down opposite him and explained her fears. Fascinated by the challenge, Mathew agreed to help, explaining that if Maddy had 'stepped into' Zara, then she was only there temporarily, and for a reason. Having been reassured by him that Zara was not being possessed or being misused, Izzy agreed to take Mathew over to visit the Pink Villa, to determine if what she believed was true. Her challenge now was setting up a meeting in Majorca.

Chapter 19

Zara left Izzy's gallery and wandered slowly back along the cobbled street. She found a coffee bar in which to sit and watch the milling visitors. Too much had happened recently and the latest revelations were still too raw and unbelievable for her to fully process. Her mobile vibrated on the table beside her. She glanced at the screen, saw Gareth's name and ignored the call. At this moment, her mind was swimming with all things unpleasant and she needed time to collect her thoughts. One coffee became two, then a brandy.

Zara remained safely cocooned by the happy, smiling crowds until the evening drew in and the walls of the old Ibiza town came to life, sparkling under the moonlight and lighting. A juggler, tossing small battery-operated globes for the public's enjoyment and potential sales, wound around her as she made her way back to the port where a water taxi, half full, sat ready for departure. She climbed on, and sitting up in the cool of the night out on the outer deck, she allowed the surrounding darkness to help hide her tears and darker thoughts.

Oh, my poor Maddy. What sort of life must you have had? she thought.

A drunken student fell across the deck, scrambling for a hold as his friends picked him up, laughing.

I wonder how much laughter you really had in your short life, she asked herself.

'Ah! But I found love, Zara. Real love. Yours, Izzy's and my own daughter's. Not everyone experiences that, my darling,' whispered Maddy.

As the water taxi left the harbour, Zara clutched her handbag tightly to her chest, Maddy's journal and phone safely tucked deep within, and enjoyed the rocking sensation of the vessel's movement. She watched as the lights from the dock grew larger and brighter. Tomorrow, Gareth would help her with the answers she now needed. Tomorrow, she would start to unravel the mess and make things right for Maddy. Tonight, she needed to pretend she knew none of what she'd read and been told. That way, she could make it through to the following morning. As the water taxi made its short docking, she alighted. With a head full of purpose, Zara strode off to the taxi rank. Airport next stop, where Majorca and Gareth waited for her.

Chapter 20

Zara curled up in bed beside Gareth, tucking herself as close to his body as sleep allowed. She knew she wouldn't sleep much herself but ached for the comfort of his closeness to help her make it through the night. She knew in the morning they would have to talk and the conversation would not be a comfortable one.

Early the following day, just as the sun soaked through their fine bedroom curtains, Zara told Gareth she had some disturbing news. Gareth listened without interruption, his face as bloodless as Zara's. 'So,' he started, unsure of where this would now take him, 'you're telling me Maddy intended to leave the day after our engagement party, with Pippa, to join Izzy?'

'Yes,' Zara replied quietly, dropping her face into her hands.

'Do you …?' Gareth stopped as he waited for Zara to lift her face to him. 'Do you think Jon could have done something … to prevent her … and it all went horribly wrong?'

'I don't know,' she whimpered.

'Well at least we understand more now,' said Gareth, dropping Maddy's mobile back onto the bed, as if letting go of the object would separate him from the unpleasant decisions to come.

'There's even more in here.' Zara passed over Maddy's journal, open at the offending page for Gareth to see.

Silently he read, his shoulders drooping more with every sickening word on that page. Lifting his head, his eyes blazed with anger. 'You need to fly back now and speak to Nathan. I'll stay on here and ensure your mother and Pippa are not left alone.'

'What do we tell Mum?' she asked, her mouth dry.

'Nothing … yet. I'll take you to the airport. Leave your suitcase here, use a carry-on. Book yourself onto the next flight to Gatwick, and when you arrive take the car straight to Nathan. He needs to answer some questions fast before we involve the police.'

Zara fumbled with her phone. 'There's an easyJet flight with spaces at twelve thirty. Can we make it?'

'Yes,' Gareth answered, already collecting his wallet and keys as Zara hastily threw her wash kit and make-up into a holdall. 'You have to.'

Climbing into the car, Zara threw her handbag onto the back seat. 'Do you have everything you need?' Gareth asked.

'Yes.'

'Good. Then let's go before Lisa and Pippa wake up. With luck, I'll get back in time for lunch. I can explain that Michael needed to see you regarding an estate matter.'

'Oh, God, I hate all these lies,' said Zara.

Gareth's face remained impassive as they drove away from the villa and up onto the main road. 'Maddy's left us no choice, Zara.'

Gareth turned his head briefly, seeing the anxious look on Zara's face and the pained look in her eyes. 'I think the few lies we have to tell now, to protect Lisa and Pippa, will be forgiven. It's what's been hidden before that concerns me.'

'Let's just hope it's not as bad as we think.'

'Somehow, Zara, I don't think we will be that lucky.'

Zara shivered as they turned off the main stretch and into the airport lane.

'I think', Gareth continued, 'it will be far worse.'

Chapter 21

Later that same evening, in his home in Cuckfield, Nathan, having just spoken to Zara on the phone to arrange a meeting, came to a decision. Nursing a large Scotch, he knew it was time to speak out, tell the truth: all of it – before it was too late, and matters got even worse. How he wished, for the millionth time, that that night in his youth had never happened. How he wished he could have turned the clock back, or owned up to his part in the whole sordid affair, but his *God* was not that kind; nor was Jon. His punishment would be to live with the guilt and knowledge of what they had all done, and dance the devil's tune forever. Because for Nathan, Jon was surely a devil.

Leaning back into the cushions of his settee, he shivered at the memory. She'd probably be married with children by now ... if ... The image of her young, lovely face punched through the haze of time, still perfect, still haunting, still waiting. 'Oh, God!' he cried, dropping his head into his hands. 'I'm so sorry, so sorry, Rachael.'

In his safe, he had a file filled with newspaper cuttings of the missing Irish girl. A Detective Martin Nesbitt had been assigned to the case and Nathan kept all the articles written about him too. He'd also collected pieces about a number of other missing children, all unsolved and handled by the same detective – innocent faces staring out from the newspapers, begging to be found. According to Detective Nesbitt, the missing children were all unlikely to be runaways and therefore their disappearance was potentially linked to something more sinister, like a paedophile ring. Nathan suspected he knew of one such ring.

During his years in practice, Nathan had received a number of calls from Jon asking for his professional input in confidence. Nathan would be collected and driven to a private address. Afterwards, he would be driven back home. His payment would be in an envelope, in cash. Nathan knew the rules: he never asked questions; he never saw anything or heard anything. There had been a number of callouts to Wimbledon, after some of Jon's dinners and private film showings in his den, normally to treat high blood pressure and ligature injuries. These took place away from the property when Tilly was alive, and then, after her death, when the housekeeper had time off. On a number of occasions, Nathan thought he saw a distinguished familiar-looking face, or a glimpse of a well-known figure as his furtive driver helped him into a tinted-windowed limousine. Nathan even believed he had seen a prominent local councillor, which would have explained the ease with which Jon had been able to sway a whole private-school board to allow Maddy time off.

It wasn't that Nathan didn't care; he cared very much. But as long as Maddy was unhurt, he kept his counsel. He too had sinned, after all. And he justified his guilty silence with the money and freedom it gave him to save as many damaged lives as he could – because on weekends and in his spare time, Nathan gave free medical treatment to a number of organisations. Still, despite all that, those grotesque silver monkeys on his desk were an ongoing reminder of that fateful night and their pact.

Now, however, relieved by his resolution to speak the truth, Nathan retired to his bed, his mind, for once, less cluttered; his soul less burdened. Wrapping the sheets around himself, Nathan attempted to block out the usual night-time images, praying for the strength to handle whatever tomorrow would bring.

Shortly before 2 am, Nathan awoke with an excruciating pain and pressure in his chest. Realising he was in trouble, he picked up the phone and called for an ambulance.

Chapter 22

A nurse answered Nathan's phone, informing Zara of his collapse, and his admission to hospital. Having made a few calls, Zara got into her car, tossed her mobile onto the passenger seat and drove to the Royal Marsden Hospital, where Nathan had been transferred to a private wing specialising in cancer treatment. Lying under the thin hospital blankets he looked frail, the cancer and guilt both eating away at him. As Zara entered his room, she recoiled at his gaunt appearance. She wondered if he would have the strength to answer her questions and help them.

Zara and Gareth needed Nathan to confirm what they believed to be the truth. They had copies of Maddy's and Pippa's DNA results and they had her journal. The final sickening question for Nathan was, were they right? Was Jon, Pippa's biological father? Zara knew her mother could never ask Nathan this; it was up to her.

Approaching the hospital bed, she smiled at its occupant, realising that what she discovered today would destroy her mother and potentially put an end to the future of their family.

'Hello, Zara,' said Nathan, looking up, his voice thin and reedy.

'Hello, Nathan. How are you feeling?'

'Not bad. Could be better, looks like the big "C" is in a hurry now.'

Zara winced at the 'C' reference. 'How long have you known?'

'Known?' A flutter of panic flashed in Nathan's eyes as they met hers.

'About the cancer?' she prompted.

'Ah. Some time.'

'Is it treatable?' she asked, placing her handbag under the chair beside the bed as she sat down.

'No. Not now, too advanced,' he told her.

'Why didn't you do something earlier? You're a doctor too.'

Nathan chuckled; he felt the cancer to be a justifiable punishment for all he'd chosen to hide. 'I knew what the treatment would be, Zara. I prefer to go on my terms, with my chosen medication. Anyway, I'm still here. Not dead quite yet!'

Zara looked at the fragile man in the bed beside her, her heart heavy knowing the truth she sought. 'I know why Maddy made me Pippa's guardian,' she told him.

Nathan pulled himself up higher onto the pillows to get a better view of Zara, turning his head slightly to one side as he briefly closed his eyes. 'Go on.'

'I know all about Maddy's childhood. Patrick Darcy wasn't Pippa's father, was he?'

'No,' Nathan answered. 'Patrick Darcy was in love with Jon.'

'Patrick!' moaned Maddy. 'My gentle soul, my confidant. What did I do to you in telling you what happened to me?' Maddy's suffering was seeping into Zara.

'Did he tell you that?' asked Zara, shocked by yet another revelation.

'Jon did. He told me Patrick was a confused young man coming to terms with his own sexuality. His parents had asked Jon to help him.'

'And in "helping" him, did that mean he abused him too?'

Nathan paused before answering. He knew the truth of the role Patrick had played back in Wimbledon, and perhaps the real reason he'd taken his own life. He'd heard the reference to Patrick being the best video prodigy to date. Nathan knew who had used him, and for what, and the thought made him shudder. 'It would have been a classic case of transference, Zara. Very common with therapists and their patients. Patrick may have fallen in love with Jon, or developed an erotic attraction towards him. This would have made him especially vulnerable should Jon have chosen to take advantage.'

Maddy's pain was unbearable. 'He must have been in such emotional agony, and I only added to it, destroying his dreams.'

Zara's face betrayed her emotions. 'And did he?' she probed.

Nathan turned his head again, closing his eyes as if to shut down the images. 'Yes,' he whispered.

Maddy sobbed within Zara, the true nature of Patrick's abuse reconnecting with her.

'Sometimes, some things are best left in the past,' began Nathan. 'Especially those you can't do anything about. The truth can sometimes do more damage than you realise. Maddy knew that.'

'But why couldn't you do something about it?' demanded Zara.

'It was … more complicated back then.'

'And now?' Zara insisted. 'Maddy left me a journal. It explains about her childhood. And there are copies of DNA results for herself and Pippa. There's also another DNA result in there …'

Nathan's head dropped back into the pillows.

'He abused her as a child and I believe he's also Pippa's father. Am I right?'

'Maddy never told me,' Nathan replied weakly.

'Could you confirm it by looking at *all* the DNA results?'

Nathan nodded. 'Who gave you all of this?'

'Izzy. Maddy's girlfriend out in Ibiza. Michael put me in

touch with her. It turns out Maddy *deliberately* left her phone with Izzy, and the journal – *in case* something should happen to her.'

Nathan took in the emphasised words as Zara briefly described her meeting with Izzy in the shop in Ibiza.

'So, little Maddy found love, after all,' said Nathan, a smile of genuine happiness lighting his face. 'I'm so pleased.'

'Why did you let all those things happen to Maddy?'

There was a pause as Nathan allowed her words to sink in. 'I never allowed myself to imagine what may be taking place. It was easier that way. I didn't want to know. He promised me she was … "untouched" by his interests.'

Zara pulled a tissue from her handbag and blew her nose. 'Well, he lied.'

Nathan's head fell back onto the pillows. He was close to tears. 'Paedophiles are experts at deception. How do you think they get away with all the unspeakable things they do? It's because no one believes them capable of such acts. Did you ever imagine Jon could commit such horrific crimes, all those years under the same roof with him and Maddy?' asked Nathan.

Zara shook her head. 'No, and she never told me. I never guessed. If anything, Jon seemed to keep his distance from Maddy.'

'He never forgave her for getting pregnant. That's why he made the decision to take her baby away and bring it home as someone else's child. A punishment,' Nathan admitted.

Zara shivered with disgust.

'Maddy would never tell on Jon,' he went on. 'Remember, despite what happened to her, he was her father. She only had him before you and Lisa came along.'

'Then her loyalties were misplaced,' said Zara.

'That's the power the abuser has over a child. She only had

117

him. She would have loved him whatever he did to her. And there are many levels of sexual abuse, Zara, not just the obvious.'

Zara began to cry quietly. The image of Maddy defenceless against Jon's advances made her feel sick.

Nathan continued. 'Maddy would have loved her father in a confused manner, and as she grew up and realised all the things done to her were not normal acts of parental love – and wrong – that's when self-doubt and guilt would have come into play. She may even have blamed herself for what happened.'

Maddy shrank deep within Zara, remembering the muddled and mixed emotions. 'I did blame myself, Zara. I thought my baby had died because I was bad.'

'No. Jon was at fault, not Maddy. But why didn't she tell me? I loved her. I would have done anything for her.'

'I told Patrick what had happened to me and he killed himself, Zara. I was never going to risk losing you and Pippa too,' whispered Maddy.

'Why? Fear that you might judge her?' suggested Nathan. 'Shame? Who knows what emotions must have played around her head. Shame is a powerful force, Zara. She was also Jon's daughter; honour and blood blur all the lines. And remember, Jon's a persuasive man. To a child, well … she wouldn't have had a chance. Plus, Jon understands the psyche. He knows how to play mind games with the vulnerable. Once he gets into your head, he can plant anything: fear, guilt, shame, duties. *I* should know.'

'So tell me, Nathan. What did Jon have on you? What made you turn a blind eye to what may have been happening and involve yourself in the cruellest of his plans – taking Maddy's baby away from her?'

Nathan shut his eyes tight, the facts too horrific to admit. 'It was fear, guilt and a pact I made back in med school. I did something unspeakable, back then. And Jon helped cover it up.

I swore never to speak of it, to protect the others involved, but as time passes I see the rules have changed. And my fear only makes Jon stronger.'

'What did you do that was so awful, Nathan? So bad that Jon used it to his advantage – then and now?'

Nathan looked up at Zara, her anger clearly registering. 'I need to start at the beginning,' he told her. 'You won't like what you are about to hear. You will hate me and you will never forgive me. When I'm done, it will be up to you to decide how much of the truth you wish to take forward.'

Zara pulled her chair closer to the bed and looked closely at Nathan. His face was pale and waxy and there were sweat beads above his lip. 'Are you well enough to do this?' she asked with genuine concern.

The eyes looking back at her were dark and shiny with unshed tears. 'Yes. I'm tired of living with this, Zara, and I don't care any longer what happens to me. I'm dying, anyway. In fact, if they incarcerate me for some of the things I'm going to tell you, I shall be happier than I've ever been as a free man. I've never truly been free. Jon has always reminded me of that. I've wanted to do this forever, Zara – tell the facts. But I couldn't. I was afraid to. Now I have nothing left to lose. The burden of truth will be in your hands. But are you still sure you want to hear it?'

Zara felt her heart skip a beat as her eyes met Nathan's.

⟜

'It all happened so long ago,' began Nathan. 'Jon, Jimmy and myself, three young men, all wanting the best that life could offer, studying and playing hard. The adventurous youth can be dangerously irresponsible, Zara, with little care for the consequences, especially when seeking their own carnal pleasures. That heady mix of sexual desire, experimentation and fulfilment, combined with the delights of easily accessible drink and drugs made everything all the more intoxicating. We were young; mad with lust and alcohol.'

Nathan remembered the comfortable lack of guilt back then, their growing sense of power, their conceit in justifying what they did with their physical satisfaction and amusement. How easily their misguided youth erased all sense of morality or accountability. How stupid they had all been.

'Jon and I met at medical school, both qualified junior doctors in our chosen speciality fields. Jimmy was a young, flamboyant London photographer. We were all high that night – high on possibilities or whatever substance had been procured. We'd taken Rachael up to a rented room in Soho. I remember it was a seedy room with a brown polyester bedspread and orange, swirly, shagpile carpet. We didn't care about the décor; it was the sex we were after. All three of us had taken it in turns to "do" the little redhead. Out of her head on vodka and promises, Rachael O'Leary, fresh off the boat from Ireland, did everything we asked. Jon poured the drinks, slipping a small tablet into her glass. I can even recall the words of his toast that night as he passed the glass to Rachael. He was right. That was a night to remember.' Nathan paused as his memory replayed the tragic event. 'We laughed that night, Zara. Oh, how we laughed, foolishly, the three of us and the beautiful young redhead. Only she started to become floppy. "Pliable," Jimmy called it. "Easier to position." I have to admit we'd arranged similar nights before without any problems. The girls never remembered the details; they were always looked after and everyone had fun. Or so we told ourselves.'

Zara's horrified expression stared back at Nathan, her hand over her mouth.

'Do you want me to continue?' he asked. 'I did warn you, but it might help you to understand if I tell you how it all started. No excuses, Zara. The truth, as you wanted.'

Zara inhaled deeply, nodding for Nathan to continue.

'Jon was the organiser, the one with the outrageous ideas,' said Nathan. 'He found the girls. The younger the better. Jimmy, as a trainee fashion photographer, would take the pictures on Jon's directions, positioning the girls' bodies into various poses. I was young, Zara, under the influence of raging hormones and drink. Not an excuse but … And I admit, back then, I found that the *setting of the scenes* turned me on badly. I forgot about the immorality of what we were actually doing. The girls were always safe, and they were consenting adults, or so they claimed; it was purely the outrageous sex that was on my mind during those sessions. The photos and recordings were for Jon's collection.'

'He took photos of me too,' Maddy whispered. 'He showed them to me one day when I wasn't doing what he wanted, threatened me with them. The camera is cruel, Zara. It can do more damage in some ways than the knife.'

'Jon never took drugs on those nights,' Nathan continued. 'Even his intake of alcohol was deliberately low. He got high on the planning and implementation. Jon wanted the photos of the girls more than the girls themselves. He said he could relive the moments that way, spend more time with the girls whenever he wanted, or share with others … for a price. On that fateful night, Jimmy had taken his best photos because he felt so sexually aroused – including some of me having sex with the girl.' Nathan paused, his face drained emotionally. 'Nobody foresaw what was about to happen. Nobody expected her to die.'

'Oh my God,' mumbled Zara, her body instinctively shrinking away from Nathan's.

'We were in shock, I remember. It was terrifying. We were traumatised and frightened by what had happened, and although I wanted to inform the authorities, Jon took total control of the situation, reminding me that not only had I supplied the drugs, but that I was the one on top of Rachael as she drew her last breath. Jimmy too was implicated; both on film and by the filming of the sex act. Jon warned us that Rachael's death could mean an end to all our careers, our reputations and our freedom. Petrified, we miserably agreed to follow his instructions. I remember how he carefully removed the camera. "A safeguard for the future," he told us. "To keep us honest with one another."' Nathan shook his head. 'He held onto the photos to keep me and Jimmy quiet, and within his control. There has been no honesty since that night, Zara.'

For Nathan, the confession was difficult, but he spoke candidly and honestly, accepting blame for his own involvement.

As horrendous as it was to listen, Zara wanted to understand what happened next. 'What did you do with the body?' she asked.

'We re-dressed Rachael …'

Zara sucked in her breath.

'Yes, we needed our exit from the hotel to look normal; it was busy that night in Soho. Jimmy and I propped her between us, each of us draping one of her arms over our shoulders. We half carried, half dragged Rachael out of the hotel and into Jon's waiting car. To the inexperienced eye we must have looked like just another group of young drunks, the worse for wear. The truth was no one was really looking and no one cared. I can still remember the fear and panic I felt as we bundled her body into the car, driving out of London towards the south. We sobered up pretty fast on that trip. Jon knew where to go. He took us to a remote stagnant river in leafy Surrey, where he parked the car. I remember how he calmly told us we needed to weigh the body down, to keep it submerged. I knew why, sickening though it was. I knew the gases formed during decomposition would lift the body to the surface.' Closing his eyes, Nathan paused, tears gathering as he did so.

'Water, Nathan?' Zara asked, her own mouth tasting unpleasant.

He shook his head, recalling a moment, before continuing. 'I saw Jon lean over Rachael and tug at a necklace around her neck, breaking the chain, before putting it in his pocket. Then he used a penknife to puncture her chest cavity, stabbing her a number of times.'

'Why?' exclaimed Zara, nauseated and unable to comprehend the unnecessary violence Nathan described.

'To allow some of the gases to escape, to help her sink.'

'Oh, God,' murmured Zara.

'Jimmy was pale-faced and shaking by then. I thought he would pass out. But Jon made us open up the hotel bedspread we'd brought with us, positioning Rachael's tiny body on it, together with some bricks we found in an abandoned van. Jon tossed in an old tyre iron for good measure to make the bundle heavier. It was me that tied the ends together.' There was a faraway look on Nathan's face as he added, 'I'll never forget the heavy plopping sound that shrouded body made when we threw it into the water, nor the cold words uttered by Jon: "We will never speak of this … and we will always look out for one another. Remember, the secret of enjoyment for everyone is to ensure there's no mess at the end!"'

'Familiar words, aren't they, Zara?' said Maddy.

Zara shivered.

'No one ever found Rachael O'Leary's body. That was over twenty-five years ago and her death still haunts me, Zara.

There's not a day goes by that I don't think of her and wish for the chance of forgiveness.'

Zara remained silent and still, the story she had just heard too horrendous to fully absorb.

⌒

What Nathan had failed to tell Zara was how he had suffered from that fateful night onwards. How he could no longer look at a girl without seeing the haunting image of Rachael's face. How his need for sex had diminished, along with his need for female contact. Applying himself to his studies, his career within the medical field assured, he'd concentrated on saving lives – the trickier the case, the better, each patient lost reminding him of that night in Soho. And he never allowed himself to become emotionally or physically attached to anyone. Something within him died that night and was buried along with Rachael's body.

For Jimmy, after the Soho incident, his career as a promising fashion photographer went into decline as his drinking increased. Terrified of being caught, he dropped out of the high-fashion world into mainstream mediocrity, photographing for a local paper under an assumed name. Until, that is, Jon pulled in a favour and turned Jimmy's world into a darker existence, behind the unseen camera of the dark web. Here, Jimmy's photographic skills proved highly lucrative. He anonymously filmed and produced pornography for a particular audience. Before long, Jimmy had put paid to any remaining qualms or discomfort about what had happened that night. Anaesthetised now to both pain and pleasure, he took dirty money to provide sexually explicit images for paying voyeurs. He would film anything that anyone wanted, for the right money. All except 'snuff movies'. He still remembered that night.

Chapter 23

Zara watched the sad expression on Nathan's tired face. For too long he had hidden his own true feelings, and as he spoke of those dreadful things, he felt his heart lifting, as if a great weight had finally been put aside. For the first time in decades, Nathan felt free of Jon's hold.

Shocked and repulsed, Zara began to understand Jon Stone's ruthlessness and the life Maddy must have endured under the same roof as him. Both openly crying now, Nathan and Zara held one another's hands, each hoping that the other's presence would lift some of the weighty darkness that his confessions had created.

After a while, Zara spoke. 'I don't forgive you for what you did back then, or how you allowed Jon to do as he wanted, but I know deep down you are an honourable and good man. Now it's time to speak out, whatever the consequences. It's not too late for Pippa or Mum.'

Nathan closed his eyes as a tear slipped down his face. He nodded.

Zara went on, 'We have full DNA test results. With these we can prove both maternity and paternity of Pippa and with that Maddy's abuse at the hands of her father.'

'They'll take Pippa away from your mother,' Nathan warned Zara.

'Not if she leaves Jon and takes Pippa with her. They can come and live with me; I'm the legal guardian.'

Nathan shook his head. 'Social services will get involved. They always do. Pippa could be taken into care; your mother will be interviewed by the police. They'll believe her complicit in all that Jon has done.'

'But that's not true!' cried Zara

'We know that. They don't. Even Pippa's adoption was never legal; they'll claim your mother knew that too.'

'But she didn't,' replied Zara. 'Look how she went to pieces when Michael told us. It won't come to that, surely. Once we expose our findings they'll investigate Jon for child abuse and incest. There's probably a whole network of contacts he knows involved.'

'Pippa can't know about Jon being her father,' begged Maddy.

'Remember, Zara, the sort of people Jon associated with were not his friends. They were influential people with the same depraved "needs". People of authority in prominent positions, high up in the police, the courts – they'll come to his aid, muddy the waters or close ranks. Maddy knew that. Jon's protected within a powerful and sickening network; a dangerous one.'

'Oh, God,' Zara said again. 'What do you suggest we do?' The reality of their vulnerability was trickling like cold water down her back.

'We need to be cautious. Lisa should know the full story, and Pippa should be protected from the truth for as long as possible. But if the police are involved and convictions made … there will be no hiding the facts of her birth. The press would have a field day.'

'Please save Pippa from the humiliation, Zara; at least until she is older and able to understand the implications,' pleaded Maddy.

'But what about the other stuff you told me about? The "deep web" and the photos of poor Patrick and Rachael O'Leary? Can't we find any of these? Surely that would be enough to get him arrested?'

'He'd have hidden those photos long ago.'

Zara's frightened expression implored Nathan for help.

'Let me speak to the police about Rachael. I know the name of the detective in charge of the original case. If we can find her body and implicate Jon, that will be a start. Who knows what else it may lead to.'

'Do you remember where she is?'

During one of Nathan's guilt attacks, he had searched for and found the disused stretch of water where Rachael's body had been dumped, the site being on a list of contaminated riverbank sites recorded by the council as 'dangerous'. Someone with powerful links and similar needs must have provided the exact location to Jon. His familiarity with the area made Nathan believe he had used this stretch of water before that night. Nathan squeezed Zara's hand. 'Yes,' he said. 'I'll never forget where we left her body. And I can provide the date and timing for Rachael's disappearance.'

Zara shivered. 'I can't believe the power this man has over people.'

'Even the dead,' murmured Maddy.

'Blackmail, fear, guilt. He is a persuasive man, Zara. Somehow, even when you know it's wrong, he finds a way to convince you it's acceptable for the good of the whole.'

'I understand,' said Zara. 'I'll speak to Mum, try and explain the DNA findings. She won't want to believe it.'

Nathan nodded. 'No, I know. Would you?'

'Not if it was someone I loved and trusted. She'll want to confront him,' said Zara.

'Jon is not a man who likes confrontation. Lisa must tread carefully as we gather all the evidence. Any knee-jerk reaction could find the authorities involved, and we must think about Pippa. Will she thank you if she loses everyone around her she loves? No, we need to take care.'

Maddy listened to their conversation. They could never understand how she felt all those years ago as a child. The dread and the fear, the supressed instinct that what he forced her to do was not right. She hated those nights the housekeeper stayed away, hated the holidays with just her father and dreaded the business meetings in his den. Even now, when he could no longer hurt or touch her, she shuddered at how he'd made her feel: exposed and helpless. After her pregnancy though, he left her alone; one small blessing. And when Pippa arrived in the household the power shifted. Jon knew Maddy watched him. While she was alive, her silence bought Pippa her safety. Now she was dead, she needed help. Pippa would be too much of a temptation for Jon.

Hearing the exchange between Nathan and Zara made her feel less helpless. But of course, they still didn't know everything; they still didn't know the truth about her death. Time was running out. Jon would be in Majorca shortly and then there would be nothing she could do to protect her daughter. She needed Zara to act now. She needed Zara to connect to her thoughts and images. To see something through Maddy's eyes, not her own. In desperation, she projected an image into Zara's mind. She showed her the moment of her fall.

Zara gasped as her body pitched forward and a vision of fast-approaching rocks flashed into her head. Clutching the bed, she snatched her breath in shock.

'Zara!' Nathan called in concern. 'Are you ok?'

Her face ashen, Zara tightened her grasp on the metal bed frame and waited for her mind to clear. She steadied herself, breathing in slowly and deeply, allowing the frightening vision to pass. 'Just a horrible thought. I'll be fine in a moment.'

'Ah! It's working, I'm getting the connection back. Keep sensing me, Zara. We are running out of time.'

Nathan had watched Zara's near collapse with professional concern. 'Have you eaten recently?' he asked.

'No, I've been too busy, but I'm fine, thank you,' Zara answered. Although in truth, she was far from fine. Her body felt disconnected and her mind filled with incoherent thoughts and pictures. 'I'm sorry but this is getting too much for me to deal with. Can you help me speak to Mum, or phone her when I'm with her in Majorca?' she asked, her face drained of any colour.

'Yes. I can do better than that. I can come out to Majorca. I want to help, Zara.'

Running her hand through her hair, Zara shook her head. 'The truth, Nathan, when it all comes out … it could mean you go to prison.' She lifted her face and stared into his eyes. 'Are you ready for that?'

Nathan smiled. 'To spend my last days in prison? I've been in a prison all my life, unable to live under the weight of this guilt, his and mine. I don't deserve any more. But tell me, does Pippa really need to know it all? Incest is not a nice word, Zara. What a stigma for her to grow up with. What would Maddy want?'

'Pippa's safety!' screamed Maddy, desperate to be heard and for them to understand her father's intentions.

Nathan stared directly into Zara's eyes and thought he caught a glimpse of something familiar looking back at him from behind the sparkling irises.

'Keep Pippa safe, Zara. Nathan's right. The whole truth for a child could be too awful to cope with. I should know. It's terrible to comprehend. But Jon can't be trusted. Pippa is at risk. He has plans.'

'Maddy would want us to keep Pippa safe,' said Zara, her breathing now back under control, the panic within her lessening. 'We can decide what to tell her as she grows older. I'm also worried about how Mum is going to take all of this. We are about to destroy her life too.'

'I know,' said Nathan, momentarily unnerved by what he'd seen fleetingly in Zara's features.

'One more thing, Nathan: do you really believe Maddy's death was a suicide?' Zara asked.

Nathan shook his head. 'No. An accident at best. She spoke to me that evening, before her fall. She was going to confront Jon with all the facts. She was leaving him to start a fresh life with Pippa. We'll never know what really happened, but I don't believe she intended to die that night.'

'What if Jon had something to do with her death?' asked Zara.

Nathan's eyes flickered with pain. 'God, I hope not.'

'On track at last ... ' Maddy's voice cried out in Zara's head.

Nathan shook his head. 'I should have stopped all of this and spoken out,' he said, lowering his head in shame.

'But it's a possibility, Nathan,' Zara continued with her train of thought. 'Maddy obviously felt threatened in some way. Why else would she have spoken to Michael about making me Pippa's guardian and left her phone and journal with Izzy for safekeeping? Why put her will in place as she did? I'm all for forward planning, but that's too coincidental. She *knew* something might happen to her.'

Nathan watched as Zara paced the hospital floor, the anguish on her face raw. 'I need to go back to the villa at once,' she told him. 'Do you really think you could make it out to Majorca? Or should I get Mum to come over to you?' she asked breathlessly.

'I'll make it. It's the least I can do,' he told her.

Zara took in Nathan's tired and strained face. 'Ok, if you're sure. Gareth is still there with Mum and Pippa, and Jon doesn't arrive until the end of next week. I can get a flight back out there later today.'

'Then you must. Go now. I'll discharge myself and tie up a few things this end before I leave. I'll join you just as soon as

I can. I'll ask Lisa if I can stay as a recuperating guest. Jon will never suspect. But we need to move fast.'

'Will they let you leave? Will you be well enough to leave the hospital and take a flight?' Zara asked, once again looking at Nathan's grey complexion, aware of his breathlessness.

'I'm a doctor. I'll be fine,' replied Nathan, relieved he had now been given the chance to put something right. *I have to be,* he thought.

Zara turned to leave then remembered the conversation she'd had with Gareth about Pippa's so-called 'adoption'. 'Just one last question, Nathan, before I go. Jon's vasectomy – do you know when he had it?'

Nathan looked up at Zara with interest. 'Vasectomy? He never had one.'

Driving to the airport, Zara was in turmoil. She knew now in her heart that Maddy's death was no accident; everything pointed to Jon. *The bastard,* she thought, *he even lied about his vasectomy.* Jon's sickening past and his ability to callously dispose of a young girl's body, manipulating others to help him, frightened her. If he could do that, what else could he do? The answers were too terrifying to consider.

Zara took her seat on the plane just as her mobile pinged with a message from Izzy. Glancing at it, she groaned – Izzy's request for an invitation to the villa being the easiest part to handle. She texted Gareth her flight details, then switched off her phone for take-off.

As the easyJet flight touched down at Palma Airport several hours later, Zara's mind still churned with unanswered questions.

'It's showtime, Zara,' whispered Maddy. *'Stay strong. I'm relying on you.'*

Chapter 24

The following morning, Zara woke next to Gareth, in her bed at the Pink Villa. Leaning back against the pillows, she looked tired and strained, having slept badly. She smiled weakly at her fiancé.

'Ok?' he asked, though he knew the answer. Zara had filled him in on Nathan's latest disturbing revelations the night before. Their conversation had lasted well into the early hours.

Zara shrugged, closing her eyes as if to shut out the inevitable.

'When's Nathan's flight due in?'

Lifting her head off the pillows to check the bedside clock, she replied, 'In about forty minutes, according to his last text. He's coming by taxi from the airport. He told me he's spoken to Mum and that she'd be getting the guest house ready for him.'

'Does she know why he's coming?' asked Gareth.

'Just that he's not been well and wanted to recuperate here in the warm weather,' replied Zara, hiding the true extent of Nathan's illness.

Gareth perched uncomfortably beside Zara. His face wore a look of concern.

'When's Jon due back out here?'

Zara shifted, then sighing, she replied, 'The end of next week.' She looked around the room and back to Gareth. 'It's not going to get any better is it?'

Gareth shook his head. 'Nope! When's Izzy due over?'

'She's already here on the island, staying with someone called Mathew on his boat in Palma.'

'God, what a mess,' said Gareth, getting up and walking towards the patio doors. There he paused, watching a small black beetle scuttle under the doorframe before opening the double doors to let it out. 'How on earth are you going to tell your mother all you've told me?'

Zara shook her head, swinging her tanned legs off the side of the bed and going over to join him. 'I've no idea.'

Pulling her close, Gareth kissed her head. 'Nathan will help.'

'Yes. But I'm afraid that what I need to cover with my mother is only half of what's to come.'

'You think there's more?' asked an anxious Gareth, regretting his question.

Zara shuddered. Within her, Maddy shifted. 'I know there's more.'

Lisa heard the taxi creep onto the driveway, the tarmac still damp from the watering system. She called out as the driver got out of the car. 'Nathan,' she said, waving. 'Watch the sprinklers!'

Nathan paid the driver and collected his small case, walking across the grass towards Lisa, a strained smile playing on his lips.

'Nathan, my darling, you should have let us collect you.'

Lisa hugged Nathan close and he felt her openness and genuine warmth. *Jon doesn't deserve these women,* he thought, untangling himself from her embrace.

Linking her arm in his, Lisa escorted him towards the guest house. 'I have your room ready – peace and quiet for you. Is there anything you need right now?'

Nathan looked around, the *whoop whoop* of the sprinklers on the lawn catching his attention. Shading his eyes, he looked up at the blue sky. 'No, I think this is all I need. Good people, a soft bed and beautiful, warm surroundings.'

'Good. Then I'll leave you to get settled, and when and if you feel like it, join me by the pool. Zara and Gareth have taken Pippa down to the beach, so it's quiet here.'

'Thank you Lisa. I'm cold, permanently cold. The warmth from the sun is all I crave now.'

'And you shall have it!' Lisa smiled. 'I'll ensure Pedro puts one of the larger umbrellas out on the patio to give you some wide shade, just in case you feel like sleeping out there. I'm so happy you asked to come out. I've also been meaning to talk to you about something that's been troubling me for some time, but I couldn't find the opportunity to ask you, especially with Jon around. There are some things I could never ask him. But it's not urgent. It can wait until you are feeling better.'

Nathan smiled warily. *And what I have to tell you is urgent and* can't *wait, but I'll try and pick my moment,* he thought, patting her hand. 'I hope we can talk honestly about anything, good or bad,' he replied.

'Thank you. I feel relieved already,' said Lisa with a smile.

Oh, my poor Lisa, you have no idea what's about to come out, thought Nathan.

Chapter 25

Zara woke early the following morning and, having assured Gareth that the meeting with Izzy was simply about Izzy's need to process Maddy's untimely death, she rushed down to the beach to meet with her and Mathew. The conversation with Lisa about Jon had yet to happen, but it wouldn't be today. Nathan and Lisa were enjoying one another's company and she now had to deal with Izzy and her unusual request to bring Mathew, a psychic and spiritual medium based in Ibiza, to the Pink Villa.

Emotionally distraught at losing Maddy, Izzy had sought comfort from Mathew. And whatever transpired during that meeting had resulted in Izzy bringing him over to Majorca to see Zara. She had been sceptical, but Izzy remained adamant that this man of hers was needed at the villa. Having gone through the 'herb-throwing' session with Emily, Zara realised that they all needed some level of closure and comfort; Izzy was no different. Her loss was as terrible as theirs, so letting Mathew onto the property was a small concession. Perhaps he could even help her; maybe he could explain why she sometimes thought she heard Maddy talking to her, or saw her face in her own reflection. Zara had put all of this down to grief and overtiredness, but the visions in her head were getting more intense. The latest one in the hospital with Nathan had frightened her; despite knowing full well that she was in a hospital in London, she had genuinely felt like she was outside the villa in Majorca, falling through the air.

So fanciful or not, this morning she woke up firmly

believing the visit from the psychic was a good thing, a necessity. Whatever Izzy's friend Mathew needed to do today, he had free reign – with Gareth looking after Pippa and her mother looking after Nathan, there was no danger of them being interrupted.

Zara walked down to the familiar jetty. The sun was round and hot even at 9.15 in the morning. Sunglasses perched on her nose, she waved as she saw the two figures in the tender turning into the *cala*.

Seeing their arrival did little to eliminate Zara's unease. Her stomach was doing cartwheels and she chewed her lip anxiously – she'd never been so unsure of anything in her life. But upon seeing Izzy's face light up with a bright and wide smile, Zara relaxed. *At least she will be happy*, she justified.

A dull and nagging ache began in Zara's lower back as she walked towards them. 'Good morning,' she said, throwing her arms around Izzy in a tight hug.

'Ready?' asked Izzy with a conspiratorial grin.

'Yes. And no,' Zara chuckled.

Izzy turned to her companion, then back to Zara, saying, 'Zara, this is Mathew; Mathew, this is Zara.'

Dressed in beige chinos, a fitted polo shirt and a pair of deck shoes, Mathew looked like any other tourist as he grasped Zara's hand. 'Hello, Zara,' he said. 'Nice to meet you. I've heard a great deal about you.'

A gentle buzz of energy pinged through Zara's hand as their flesh connected. Mathew grinned at her. 'It's starting,' he whispered, removing his peaked cap and glasses. Startled, Zara let go of his hand, automatically pulling her own tightly into her chest as she stared up at the bluest pair of eyes she'd ever seen. *Stunning,* she thought. *This blond-haired man is breathtakingly stunning!*

Aware of the effect Mathew had on most women, Izzy smiled. 'I reckon Zara thinks you should be wearing a cloak, kaftan or sandals to do this,' she said, draping her arm around Zara's shoulders and breaking the spell. 'Don't worry, he knows he looks a fraud. But trust me, you'll be pleasantly surprised.'

Mathew smirked as he jammed his cap back onto his sun-bleached hair and hid the dark-lashed eyes behind his glasses again. 'We aim not to alert or frighten the natives,' he quipped, theatrically tracing the outline of his clothing with his tanned hands. 'Find this look goes unnoticed. I've tied alongside the jetty. Hope it's not someone else's spot.'

Zara shook her head. 'No, you're fine there. Where've you come from?'

'Just the next *cala* west from here. My captain's moored the *Water Hawk* outside the entrance, more water and room to manoeuvre,' said Mathew, tipping his sunglasses down his nose to look at Zara more closely. *Those eyes*, thought Zara. *Is he going to hypnotise me because I'd gladly go anywhere with those eyes.* She smiled back, blinking to break the hold. 'I think I've seen the *Water Hawk* around the island,' she spluttered, momentarily unnerved by Mathew's good looks, his strong bone structure emphasised by his close-cropped hair. 'Is it a dark blue and mahogany yacht, very beautiful, very classic, with ornate woodcarvings on the helm? Turkish, possibly?' she asked, feeling ridiculously proud of her detailed description. It had been Maddy who had pointed out the *Water Hawk* to Zara on one of their recent sailing jaunts with Pippa. She'd forgotten about it, until just now.

Mathew smiled. 'Oh, you are good. What a sketch! But yes, it's not easily missed or forgotten. It's a gulet. I inherited it from a great uncle who believed, quite seriously, he'd been a pirate in another life.' Mathew chuckled with gentle humour. 'I charter it with my three crew members. Currently, I'm using it for the summer while I visit friends in Ibiza and here on the island.'

'It's a stunning boat. Does it stay here in the Mediterranean all year?'

Mathew nodded. 'Yes, I'm back and forth between Ibiza, Menorca, Mallorca and the Formentura islands. You should try a day with us on the boat. Wonderful way to see the coastland, and the chef's quite a find.'

'Mathew's the chef,' Izzy admitted. 'And yes, he's quite a find.'

Zara smiled in confusion. 'What do you actually *do*, Mathew? Izzy calls you a spiritual medium, but I've never met one, nor do I believe they live on boats such as the *Water Hawk*.'

'Ah … so my clever disguise has worked,' he grinned.

Flustered, Zara continued. 'I just didn't know what to expect.'

Mathew linked arms with Zara and Izzy. 'I know. And I'm definitely not what anyone expects. I've been called many things in my line of work – salty sea dog, chef, boat owner, sea gipsy, vagrant playboy, but "medium" works for me today.'

'What exactly *can* you do, then … as a medium?' Zara asked, suddenly finding the prospect of what Mathew might do less daunting and more interesting. 'Do you really speak to the dead?'

Mathew released the two girls, sat down on the narrow bank and leaned back against the stones and plants. Here, he paused, tilting his face to the sun and folding his arms. '"Communicate" would be a better way to describe what happens. Sometimes it's voices I hear; sometimes I'm aware of particular scents or smells, or I can see images, either in my mind or with my eyes. Sometimes I sense or just "know" things. I allow myself to connect on a level that lets me pick up information however it's given to me – like a radio transmitter, turning a dial until I get a channel and tuning in. Then I have to decipher what comes through.'

'Is it hard to do?' Zara asked.

'It takes some concentration,' he replied with a smile.

Izzy turned towards Zara. 'I call Mathew a "reluctant medium". He has *many* abilities, some of which he hides, but I guarantee he will be able to help here.'

Mathew nodded gratefully. 'Hopefully,' he added, his voice warm with humour.

'So how will you start?'

'I'll ask Maddy to talk to me.'

'Just like that?' asked Zara, amazed. 'Don't you need props? A board with letters?'

'That's a séance,' said Izzy.

Maddy had been listening to their exchange with renewed hope. 'Give him a chance, Zara. He's probably my only chance of getting through to you.'

Mathew smiled. He didn't mind being grilled by Zara. Blind faith was dangerous and he wanted her to ask as many questions as she needed. 'I don't have to physically talk to anyone, Zara. I use what's available to me and what works; that's clairvoyance, clairaudience and clairsentience.' With a grin, he continued. 'Sometimes I use them all at once. Whatever connects me.'

'Mathew is known as a channeller,' Izzy told Zara. He can get a non-physical consciousness to speak "through" him.'

'Izzy, you promised no spinning heads!' Zara exclaimed in panic.

'It's not like that, Zara, I promise.'

'No, it's not,' Mathew assured her, smiling at the reaction.

'Well, just as long as you don't frighten me,' cautioned Zara, looking at Mathew's kind expression. 'So what if it doesn't work and you can't speak to Maddy?' she asked.

'I'll try my best. If she wants to communicate with us – and something tells me she does, badly – she'll try to.' Mathew watched the faces of the two girls looking at him with such hope.

'Oh, but you will hear from me, I promise,' whispered Maddy. 'I just need to get someone to help me to connect.'

Standing on the rocky ground, Zara wondered whether she'd made the right decision allowing Izzy and Mathew to come. 'So where do we start?' she asked nervously, looking to Izzy for reassurance.

'Can you take me to the place where Maddy fell?' asked Mathew.

Both girls looked up at the winding pathway. 'The top or the bottom?' asked Zara.

'The top. We need to retrace the steps that led to her fall.'

Partway up the path, Mathew paused, taking one hand from each girl and holding them gently. Zara and Izzy cried out in unison and shuddered as a vibration, like a low-voltage shock, flew through them. Breaking the contact, Zara held her hand to her face in disbelief. 'What was that?' she asked.

Shaken, but amazed, Izzy examined her own hand. 'I think that was Maddy!'

Mathew, aware of the current that had flown so strongly through them, realised this might not be as straightforward as he'd thought. His job today would not be just with the dead … but very much with the living. Izzy's instinct was right. Maddy *was* 'inside' Zara. Turning towards her now, Mathew took both of her hands in his, reading the expression on her face as he looked into her eyes. 'Zara?'

She remained perfectly still, watching him closely. 'Yes.'

'What I'm going to tell you may frighten you at first, but I need you to trust me. Do you understand?'

Nodding her head, Zara smiled.

'And you, Izzy – it's vital you keep calm too.'

Izzy nodded.

'Maddy hasn't left yet,' continued Mathew. 'She's still very much here.'

Zara's head shot up, scanning the pathway and surrounding gardens. 'Where? Can you see her, sense her?' she asked with excitement.

'No … she's not out there. She's still with us … *in* you.'

Gasping for air, Zara tried to grab her hands back, but Mathew held firm in an effort to reassure her. 'I don't understand,' she cried, pulling away, as if to run.

'Zara!' Mathew called out. 'Listen to me. Maddy's not going to hurt you. She's inside you but totally unconnected to you. She chose to step into you for a reason, though, and we need to find out why. She won't hurt you,' he said again. 'I sense a lot of love there for you. We need to understand why and what she needs to tell us.'

'Oh, God,' moaned Zara, moving sideways towards the garden slope and dropping down onto the bank. 'I knew it!'

'What do you mean?' asked a distraught Izzy.

'I've seen her … in the mirror. And I've sensed her. I think she tries to talk to me, but I just thought I was going mad and so I blocked the thoughts out.'

Mathew crouched down, looking up at Zara. 'She must love and trust you very much, Zara, or she wouldn't have done that.'

'How do I get her out of me, then?' gasped Zara, her throat constricted in panic.

'We need to establish why she stepped in first,' explained Mathew, 'and why she won't leave you.'

Maddy watched Mathew through Zara's eyes. 'Don't you dare try and move me on yet. We have work still to do here.'

Frightened, Zara turned to Izzy who nodded gently, smiling back in encouragement. This had not come as a total surprise to her, but she realised how distressing it must all be for Zara and felt a little uncomfortable with actually hearing it herself.

'What happens now?' Zara asked Mathew, a slight tremor in her voice.

'I need you to sit calmly, close your eyes, relax … and allow Maddy to speak through you.'

'I can't do that!' Zara panicked, the distress obvious in her face and voice.

'Yes, you can,' Mathew calmly told her. 'I'll hold your hands, and together, we will listen to Maddy. She will use whatever way she can to communicate. It could be pictures in your mind, or words. I don't know what will work for you or how receptive you'll be.'

'Izzy!' Zara's bloodless face searched her new friend's eyes.

'It's all right, Zara. Mathew won't let anything happen to you. Remember, Maddy loves you. She just needs your help.'

'Shall we try, then?' asked Mathew.

Zara numbly nodded back, her eyes filled with apprehension.

Mathew sat down beside Zara. He took one of her hands in his, gently whispering words of love and encouragement as he did so.

Closing her eyes, she began to relax, as, within her, Maddy listened to Mathew's calming voice. Without breaking the contact, Mathew reached across Zara to take her other hand.

Aware that Mathew was now deliberately steering Zara, Maddy awaited her chance to connect.

'Maddy?' began Mathew, eyes closed, speaking out loud for Zara and Izzy's benefit, his voice full of compassion. Mathew knew that stepping into a living person would have been a desperate and frightening decision for Maddy to take and he sensed her anxiety and sadness. 'I know you can hear me, Maddy, and I know you can see everything through Zara's eyes. You know that Zara now has your journal and that she has spoken to Nathan.'

Zara felt a soft tingling sensation pulse through her body.

'That's my girl,' whispered Mathew.

Izzy watched the two of them anxiously, her thoughts a mixture of hope and fear. She knew Maddy had stayed so she could protect Pippa. She also believed her tragic death wasn't an accident. For Izzy, the idea that the girl she had loved had been forced to trap herself between life and death broke her heart. Maddy didn't deserve this. Izzy wanted Maddy to step out of Zara, to leave it to the living to protect each other. Now all she could do was watch and pray.

With Zara's eyes closed, Maddy couldn't see anyone, but she sensed Mathew's and Izzy's presence, felt his strong hands in Zara's and heard his gentle, yet commanding voice. This was the one person who could help her. Throughout her life, Maddy had silently suffered inexcusable abuse, her strength of character her only shield. She'd endured so much, waited so long for her chance at happiness. But in the end, he'd taken that too. This time, she would fight back, tell her story; death was not going to stop her. Summoning every ounce of willpower within her soul, Maddy connected. Her voice, strong and true, reached Mathew through Zara. Both heard the words clearly within their own heads.

'I'm here, Mathew.'

Zara sobbed, straining at Mathew's hands. Holding onto her tightly, Mathew nodded for Izzy's benefit. 'We hear you, Maddy.'

'Oh, God. Thank God,' murmured Izzy, her voice choked with raw emotion.

Mathew coaxed Maddy to continue. 'We know about your childhood, Maddy, how you suffered, and what your father did to you.'

Both Zara and Mathew heard a sob, felt the stab of emotion within their own guts. They were experiencing Maddy's own feelings, sharing her pain.

'We want to help you to leave now,' said Mathew, glancing over at Zara. She sat, shoulders hunched, one hand in his, the other now held tightly across her body, as if protecting herself from the wave of sickening dread that washed through her.

'I can't leave yet. You need to understand what he's capable of.'

Zara shivered. She hadn't told either Izzy or Mathew of Nathan's confession, but she and Maddy both knew the dreadful story of that night in Soho when Rachael died. She had a very good idea of what Jon was capable of.

'He took my future,' Maddy whispered.

At these sad words even Mathew found his composure weakening. 'He can't hurt you now. We'll look after everything for you. Pippa is safe.'

A feeling of relief flooded their bodies. Mathew took Zara's other hand again, and Maddy's connection grew stronger. She wasn't letting either of them go now. 'What happened to you on the night you fell?' Mathew asked Maddy.

Izzy and Zara both held their breath, waiting for an answer. At first, Zara thought she'd gone, then Maddy sent a powerful rush of heat through their bodies, making both Zara and Mathew cry out. Zara's eyes opened wide in astonishment as she waited for the butterflies in her stomach to subside, wondering if the sickening thuds in her heart were her own or a symptom of Maddy's distress. Izzy's beautiful face looked at her in alarm.

'Did you feel that?' asked Zara, squeezing Mathew's hands tighter.

'I think she's trying to communicate something frightening to us. Her use of body temperature is to show us her fear. We have a powerful link to Maddy, but it's important we trust her.

She has something important to tell us about that night. I'm going to encourage Maddy to "show" us what happened. Keep holding my hands and allow Maddy to guide us. Are you ok with this, Zara?'

Zara nodded, her breath coming short and fast. Mathew squeezed her hands. 'Just stay with me and listen to my voice. I'll be here with you all the time. Keep remembering, Maddy loved you very much. She won't do anything that could hurt or frighten you.' Mathew smiled briefly then closed his eyes as he directed his question to Maddy: 'Show us the evening of your death, Maddy.'

Mathew and Zara, their fingers entwined, waited for Maddy's input. When Maddy connected this time, the sensation was not unlike a mild electrical current flowing through their bodies, less violent than the wave of heat they'd experienced earlier. There was no discomfort, just a pulsing sensation as energy from one person bled into another. Zara opened her eyes and looked incredulously at both Izzy and Mathew.

'I can feel something within me!' she exclaimed. 'I can see pictures in my mind.' As the images formed in her head, Zara relaxed. With her acceptance, the clarity and definition improved. It was like watching a home movie; she could clearly see the surrounding gardens, the pathway down to the jetty and beach. Looking down, she saw her toenails: blue nail varnish!

'Wait,' Zara cried, opening her eyes to temporarily break the connection. 'I don't wear blue nail varnish.'

'It's mine,' replied Maddy. 'I can only give you the images that come from my eyes, my body, the emotions too. You will be walking in my shoes, Zara. Do you want me to go on?'

Zara paused for a moment. Mathew nodded his head in encouragement, squeezing her hand in commitment. 'Yes,' she answered, 'I can feel you … walking.'

'Our connection is good then, Zara. Are you sure still? It's not a happy memory.'

Zara held onto Mathew's hands more tightly. She'd gone this far, the whole truth was so close and she owed it to Maddy. 'I'm ok, Maddy. I'm ready ... to be you.'

Izzy watched as Zara closed her eyes. Bravely taking that final and difficult leap of faith, Zara experienced again that overwhelming mixture of hope and fear. Something was going to be revealed today, that would alter tomorrow, forever.

Chapter 26

Eyes closed, Zara breathed in deeply, allowing the emotions and pictures to flood her very being. It was as if *she* had stepped inside of Maddy, not the other way around, and she could sense and see every detail through her eyes.

She sat on the jetty, her beautiful pale yellow dress bunched up under her bottom and tucked between her thighs, her tanned legs and feet dangling down towards the water as she watched the Phoenix *gently rocking on the milky-grey water, so pretty in the moonlight. Above her shone the full moon, so bright, so welcoming. A sense of peace filled her body and she smiled. Not long now, she told herself. Beside her were her delicate, strappy high heels. She'd done all she could do now, her boat already stacked with provisions and ready for their trip. A sense of sadness washed over her for her lost childhood, and those stolen years when she could have spent time with Pippa as her mother. She knew her departure tomorrow would hurt those she loved, but she had no other option. One day soon, she'd return to the Pink Villa; it was rightfully hers and it would be what her grandmother wanted.*

Feeling a sense of relief and surprise, she thought back to that meeting with her father. It had gone better than she'd expected. He knew by contesting her rights that he would incriminate himself. Drawing her feet back onto the jetty, she tucked her arms around her knees, a single tear slipping down her face. Shaking her head in sorrow, she swore it would never happen again, not if she could help it, and not to her Pippa. Loosening her arms from her body, she looked at her precious dress, frowning at the creases, as she stood proud on the deck, her wet feet leaving dark footprints against

147

the bleached wood. For a moment, she wavered, thinking of the damage and heartache she would cause both Lisa and Zara. Then, looking up at the moon, she drank in its gentle glow. The smell of the salt air filled her nostrils; so too the subtle traces of scent from the garden's pine and bougainvillea, blowing in the soft breeze.

A hesitant smile played on her mouth as she turned to leave the water, beginning the journey up to the villa and a new start.

As Zara and Mathew sat, their hands clasped, Maddy showed and shared with them all the beauty she'd loved: her boat, the sparkling water in the *cala*. They felt her new-found sense of relief and snatched happiness. They walked with her, back from the beach towards the gardens, feeling the uneven ground beneath her feet, both consciously aware of all her excitement and expectations, up to the place where it all changed.

Jon's sudden appearance from out of the garden bushes startled them. Sensing Maddy's alarm, Mathew and Zara recognised what was about to be revealed, but they could only helplessly watch the scene unfold through Maddy's eyes, and share *her* terror. When Maddy showed them what came next, Zara screamed, breaking the connection.

Tears ran silently down Zara's face as she sat, numbed with shock, hugging herself tightly. Beside her, Mathew, his eyes betraying his own feelings, struggled with what he'd just experienced. Together, they'd shared every emotion Maddy had felt that night, and now, sitting close to where she had fallen, it felt as if their own bodies had been physically assaulted and thrown onto the rocks below. They too had felt the intensity and violence of Jon's hatred, that terrifying moment of Maddy's futile realisation, the horrifying sensation of falling through the air and the contact with the rocks below. Apart from the dull thud. They were spared that pain because Maddy had stopped sharing the physical with Mathew and Zara at the point of impact, the shock alone being enough to break their connection.

Zara cried softly, covering her face with her hands as she sobbed. 'Poor Maddy. Poor, poor Maddy,' she whimpered, as Mathew, his eyes brimming with unshed tears, looked over towards the edge where she'd fallen. The detailed images she'd shown them – so clear, so powerful – were spinning frantically through his mind. He shivered in shocked fear, loosening a single tear. Izzy, protected in part from the obvious distress experienced by Mathew and Zara, crouched white-faced in front of them both. 'What did she show you? What happened?' she asked, frightened by their distraught expressions.

Zara lifted her face from her hands to look at Izzy, streaks of mascara running down her pale cheeks. 'Maddy didn't jump or fall, Izzy. She was thrown to her death.'

Izzy caught her breath, her aching heart feeling as if it would literally implode. Turning to Mathew in misery, she asked the question nobody had yet answered: 'Jon?' she whispered.

Mathew nodded, his voice unable to carry the words.

Izzy sighed deeply, the violent thumping in her chest becoming a persistent flutter. 'So it *was* murder, then?'

'Yes,' answered Mathew, clearing his throat before continuing. 'He grappled with her, throwing her off the pathway and over the side onto the rocks.'

'Oh my God!' Izzy's face registered stark fear. 'Can we prove it?'

Mathew and Zara exchanged looks. 'No,' said Mathew, shaking his head. 'He threw her just far enough away to make it look like a fall or a jump. With no witnesses and no motive, we only have Maddy's account; and that's obviously inadmissible.'

'So her death will be recorded as an accident. Jon gets away with murder?' asked Izzy.

Zara looked at Mathew. 'So that's why she stepped into me; to tell us what happened to her and to protect Pippa. She couldn't leave knowing the past and future intentions of her own father.'

The group sat for a moment in silence, their jumbled emotional thoughts with the murdered Maddy. Zara, her stomach still twisting in knots, looked across at the others. 'I can still feel her,' she softly told them. 'I can hear, sense and smell everything she wants to show me,' Zara admitted, shivering with distress. 'Can I switch her off?' she whispered, looking at Mathew. 'Or am I going to be permanently connected to her, day and night?'

'Not sure,' said Mathew, conscious that Maddy may not be able to leave, and that that in itself would create further difficulties for Zara. 'Ask her to be respectful, and only connect when necessary. Imagine her on the end of an open telephone line – there, but only when you wish to pick up the receiver.'

'Will that work?' asked Zara.

Mathew wasn't entirely sure himself, Maddy's need to communicate being obviously very powerful. 'Ask her,' he suggested.

'I know how to be discreet, Zara,' whispered Maddy. 'Just let me switch on to you when necessary.'

Zara shivered again. 'When do you think she stepped into me?' she asked.

'At the moment of her death.'

'In the hospital, then?'

Mathew nodded.

'I don't know what's more frightening – the knowledge that she's inside of me or the realisation that Jon is a murderer and capable of anything. As much as I love Maddy and want to help, I'd prefer it if she found a way to leave me.'

'I'm sorry, Zara. I had no choice. The power of a mother's love knows no bounds. Not even death can get in its way.'

'Now we know what really happened, couldn't we get her death reinvestigated?' asked Zara, hesitating as Maddy's voice cut through her own thoughts.

'No! You can't very well tell the Guardia Civil you witnessed my death via a psychic connection encouraged by Mathew, or that the victim is currently residing in your own body, and now speaking to you.'

Zara dropped her face into her hands and groaned.

'Anyone other than Izzy and Mathew will think you've lost your mind if you tell them I'm inside you,' added Maddy.

'Zara?' asked Mathew, watching her. 'Are you all right?'

Zara smiled weakly. 'She's warning me not to tell anyone about her "residing" in my body. She's concerned they'll think I've lost my mind.'

Despite the tension, Izzy grinned. 'She's still got her sense of humour, then?'

Zara smirked uncomfortably as Maddy continued to communicate.

'It's all a bit dark, Zara. We need black humour or we'll never get through it. I'm sorry,' she said again. *'I needed to protect Pippa. Jon wants her as a replacement for me ... and that's not just on a parental level.'*

Zara's face crumpled with the distressing image.

'The first step is to take Pippa away from harm, show Lisa the journal. Nathan can help explain the genetic systems and markers for the DNA results; all conclusive evidence that my father is Pippa's father too.'

Zara nodded her head. 'We will. But it's going to destroy my mother.'

'I know, and that's something I wish I could avoid. But unless

you tell her and get Pippa away from my father, he will step over that line and then there's no going back. The man has no morality and believes he's above the law. I know the frustration, Zara,' Maddy continued, *'but you must stay strong for me now. My death may still be recorded as accidental, but that doesn't matter. We know the truth. And we must protect Pippa.'*

Mathew and Izzy watched Zara as Maddy's thoughts flooded her mind.

'What is she telling you?' asked Izzy,

'To tell Mum about Pippa's parentage, get her safely away from Jon.'

'Once Lisa knows the truth and Pippa is safe, will Maddy be able to leave you?' Izzy asked, looking to Mathew for the answer.

'It's up to Maddy to choose her moment to leave,' he told her.

'That's if someone tells me how I'm supposed to do it,' added Maddy, to herself.

⁓

Mathew took his leave, tracing his way back down to the jetty, taking his dinghy back to the *Water Hawk* – back to his crew and normality, of sorts. The channelling received from Maddy had been one of the most powerful and unsettling he'd ever experienced. Warning Zara that the communication mechanism between herself and Maddy might now only get stronger, he had some concerns as to how she would cope. His parting words were, 'Call me any time. I'm not far away.'

Arms linked, Zara and Izzy made their way back up to the garden. Safely back at the top, they watched Mathew turn west out of the *cala* towards the larger bay.

'We're on our own now, Izzy,' said a dazed Zara. 'Apart from Maddy, obviously.'

Chapter 27

Detective Martin Nesbitt replaced the phone in its cradle, a faint smile on his time-worn face. Opening his laptop, he pulled up his notes for one particular missing person's case. The call he'd just received from Majorca may have been the breakthrough he'd been waiting for, for most of his career.

A sense of anticipation washed through his body as he scrolled through the records that he knew so well. The caller had given him information that was not in the public domain, convincing Martin it was genuine and that he must have met Rachael O'Leary on the night of her disappearance. The caller maintained that Rachael had died accidentally, electing not to disclose the exact manner and nature of her death for the time being. But he did tell Martin where her body could be found. Martin checked the details of the location he gave; it existed as described – a stretch of wasteland off a contaminated river, owned by the council and closed to the public. Straightening his tired frame, adrenaline pumping through his body, he punched the air. Perhaps this would bring to an end the mystery that had haunted Martin for most of his years in vice.

Rachael O'Leary's disappearance had become something of an obsession for Martin. He was now fifty-five and hardened by what he'd seen and investigated over his years in the force, but, in his mind, Rachael always remained as young and lovely as she did in the photo her mother gave him: a beautiful girl, full of potential.

With no communication from her daughter, and no sightings

from the police or public, Sara O'Leary had travelled from Ireland to London to plead for help in finding her daughter, Rachael. That was when Martin, then a young officer in the Metropolitan Police, had first met her; and, over the years, the two of them kept in touch. She never gave up on her daughter. And neither did he.

Sara O'Leary couldn't forgive herself for allowing her daughter to travel to London by herself. Rachael had been communicating with a photographic agency based in the city, who'd suggested she come over with a view to modelling for a young women's catalogue company. Sara read the invitation letter and checked out the company in question. It had all looked perfectly genuine, so an interview was set up and arrangements made for Rachael to stay with her brother, Sean, a twenty-one-year-old builders' mate working on a historic-building renovation in Piccadilly. Sean had digs outside of London in Clapham and caught a lift into town each day with one of the team on the job. He'd happily undertaken to look after his sister and see she made it to and from her interview.

On the day of her disappearance Rachael had dressed in a blue skirt and matching jacket, a pair of brown high-heeled shoes – newly purchased and higher than she normally wore – and carefully done her hair and makeup. She looked so beautiful, Sean said he felt his heart would burst with pride for his little sister. As a gift, he'd placed around her slender neck a silver necklace on which a tiny heart hung. The heart had a secret catch that opened to reveal another tiny heart, which also opened, and within it sat an even smaller gold heart. The intricate charm, bought in an old jewellery shop, was reported to have been one of a kind, made by the silversmith for fun and never sold. When Sean had explained how he wanted something unusual and special for his sister, the jeweller had allowed the charm to leave his care out of pure kindness. 'A gift layered with love,' he called it, and gladly wrapped it for Sean.

Rachael had loved the necklace, as well as the sentiment. 'I shall wear this always,' she had told her brother.

Sean proudly photographed Rachael for their mother that day, then waited excitedly for her return and news of her interview. When by 6.30 he hadn't heard from her, he had started to worry. Calling the number given to him for the photographic company, he was advised the Rachael had not turned up for her appointment, and the number they'd called her on hadn't answered. They'd assumed she had decided not to attend the interview. Distraught, Sean had trolled the surrounding cafés, the local train station and undergrounds, in an attempt to find her. There had been no sightings of her since she left that morning to catch a train. She'd vanished into thin air. The police, put her disappearance down to the 'excitement of London' and told Sean to wait – she'd turn up.

Sara refused to believe her daughter would just walk out into another city without telling a soul, and she told Martin as much. Nor did she believe Rachael was just another teenager that didn't want to be found.

Sean gave up his job, taking to the streets in the hope of finding his sister. Sara eventually returned home to Ireland a broken woman. Rachael became another missing-person statistic on the Met's books.

The photograph of Rachael that Sara left with Martin was the one taken on the day she disappeared. He still retained a copy in his personal file. The smile she gave to her brother was so hauntingly beautiful, her colouring, typically Irish – red hair, green eyes, pale, creamy skin – and an innocence that lit her face from within. 'My daughter was a good girl,' Sara had stressed.

When Martin held the photo of the young girl, he could almost hear the sound of her laughter. Around her neck he saw the heart charm. Holding the picture back then, he knew instinctively that something bad had happened to Rachael. Beautiful girls like that were noticed and not forgotten; they didn't just vanish.

Much older now, Martin worked with his team primarily on sex crimes, their investigations taking them deep within the dark web, into what he termed 'nightmare land'. Here, users surfed beneath the everyday internet using The Onion Router or Tor with complete anonymity. This was where Martin searched, looking for faces, lost children like Rachael who had made the wrong connections or taken a ride in the wrong car. Hardened by the crimes he'd investigated, Martin dug deep, convinced that one day he'd find a way to trace and punish all those sick individuals hiding behind and within the web, hoping to find that one piece of evidence – a name or a link – that would lead him to Rachael or other missing children and those responsible for their disappearance. That belief kept him sleeping at night. That, the promise he'd made to Sara – and a large dose of whisky. Martin always believed that somewhere out there was someone with a conscience and, sooner or later, they'd break and give him that little piece of evidence he needed.

Over time, his choice of career had proved costly on a personal level. His marriage couldn't survive the seedy investigations and their sordid findings. His work and his wife did not make good bedfellows and she left him after three years of marriage, citing adultery 'of sorts'. She claimed Martin was already married to his job. And 'in love' with Rachael.

When Sean O'Leary finally gave up searching for his sister, he gave up on life, choosing to die on the streets, out of work, out of luck – just another unhappy person looking for solace through the addict's needle. His mother had died ten years previously from an aggressive and painful cancer. She'd contacted Martin from the hospice in her final days, asking him to keep looking for her daughter and to bury her 'decently' should she ever be found. Martin, a lapsed Catholic, always hoped Sara and Rachael would meet up on the other side. In his line of work, he saw so much death, so much darkness; despite his wavering belief, he needed a God, and the possibility of salvation to lessen his pain.

But with the call from Majorca, Martin's spirits lifted. Climbing into his car, he drove deep in thought towards the location given by the caller. Before involving others, he wanted to find the place for himself, checking and judging the facts with the description and story given. This could be the place of Rachael's concealment or a hoax. As this case had become personal, he wanted it handled perfectly. If the lead proved solid, he'd take it to the next stage: warrants and skilled personnel to search the surrounding area and water.

Pulling up onto the unkempt and uneven ground, Martin looked around the derelict area. Among the undergrowth, he spotted the carcasses of two rusting vehicles, stripped of number plates and spilling their parts like entrails among the surrounding nettles and brambles. So far, the caller's description of the roads leading to the site and the geographical layout matched what he now saw, although shrubs and trees around the riverbank hid the water from immediate view. Despite this, somewhere within his psyche he sensed this was the place. Opening his car door, he stepped out. 'If you're out here somewhere, Rachael, I'll find you, I promise,' he murmured to the wind. 'And I'll give you that decent burial, as your mother always wanted.'

Having made the call to Detective Nesbitt, Nathan felt cold. Trembling, he moved out of his room and into the sunshine. Standing on the patio, he looked across the lawn towards the pool area where he could see Zara and another young woman greeting Lisa. *That must be Izzy,* he thought, moving towards them. *It's now or never. Time to face the truth.*

Despite his ill health, Nathan found himself walking better than he had yesterday, and his body felt stronger. *Weight lifted,* he told himself, thinking of his call to Martin Nesbitt. *I should be positively floating after my next terrible confession.*

Chapter 28

The two girls made their way over to the pool, still arm in arm, both for comfort and support. Zara introduced Izzy to her mother and Gareth, explaining that she'd come over from Ibiza on the *Water Hawk* with her friend Mathew, who'd gone back to join his crew on his boat in the next *cala* for lunch.

Pippa squealed as soon as she saw them, abandoning her wet towel in her excitement. 'Hi, Izzy!' she said, throwing herself at her legs.

Izzy laughed, separating herself from the damp child. 'Well, hello, my little golden girl,' she answered. Taking Pippa's hands, she dropped onto her haunches and pulled her close.

'I'm glad you came,' Pippa whispered, her eyes searching Izzy's face. 'I was frightened I'd never see you again.'

Izzy hugged her tighter, smelling the sun cream and chlorine in her hair. Maddy and Izzy's affair had obviously involved Pippa to an extent, although she hadn't realised the true nature of their relationship. Now, as the two of them held one another firmly, both felt their loss acutely, along with a reconnection to Maddy.

Surprised to learn that Pippa had already met Izzy, their affection for one another evident, Lisa graciously invited her to join them for lunch. The meal was a relaxed and happy affair, allowing Zara and Izzy some temporary relief from their frightening discoveries.

Zara caught Nathan's eye. *Time?* she mouthed. He bowed his head.

While Izzy entertained Pippa and Lisa cleared the table, Zara took Nathan aside, suggesting a gentle stroll around the property. Gareth, relieved from 'Pippa duty', moved back into the sitting room to check his laptop.

Arm in arm, Nathan and Zara moved away from the pool area and out towards the high pines.

'We need to tell Mum today,' Zara said.

'I know. I just wanted to enjoy her company before I destroyed her life and our friendship forever.'

'I understand, but this must be done before Jon arrives. It won't go away. We have to face it. This evening, then?'

Nathan nodded. 'This evening,' he agreed reluctantly. 'By the way, I've been in contact with the detective on the case of Rachael O'Leary.'

Zara looked puzzled for a moment.

'I spoke to him earlier today. He's going to contact me later after he's checked out my story.'

'Well done, Nathan. Tell me, does he believe you?' asked Zara.

Nathan paused. 'I know things that weren't available to the press. I gave him my name and the details of where we dropped her body. If it's still there, he'll find her.'

'Then what?' asked Zara anxiously.

'He'll need to interview me.'

'Will you tell him about the others involved?' she asked.

Nathan thought carefully before answering. 'Yes. It's time for everyone to accept their part in her death. I also think we may have some other problems coming.'

Zara looked perplexed. 'In what way?'

'I have some concerns about there being more than one body down there and I don't want to be blamed for crimes I didn't commit.'

Zara caught her breath. 'What makes you say that?'

'Something your mother said. It appears she's found some … things.'

'What things?'

'Do you remember me telling you about Jon removing a necklace from Rachael's body?'

Zara nodded, the thought sending a shiver through her.

Aware of her discomfort, Nathan lifted his head to meet those intense, toffee-coloured eyes and sighed, lowering it again slowly as he exhaled. 'Well, your mother found a collection of jewellery – broken necklaces, odd earrings, tiny rings – all tucked away in a metal toolbox in a shed at the Wimbledon house. She'd been clearing out and wanted to know what the box contained. One of the pieces inside the toolbox caught her attention. She said it was a beautiful silver locket shaped like a pair of closed wings that when opened displayed a huddled cherub; very intricate and very tiny. She removed it from the box, intending to ask Jon who it belonged to and if she could give it to Pippa.'

'And?' she prompted.

'When she mentioned the toolbox in the shed, Jon's reaction frightened her. She assumed she'd stumbled on something precious belonging to Maddy or her mother, Matilda. So she didn't mention the necklace, but when she went to replace it, the box had disappeared.'

'Perhaps the jewellery did belong to them?' suggested Zara, disturbed by where this conversation was heading.

Nathan shook his head. 'Lisa doesn't think so. Jon's response was too extreme; full of anger. After her discovery, he spent a lot of time locked away in his study and up in the loft, clearing out "things", as he put it.'

'When did all this happen?' asked Zara. 'She didn't mention anything to me.'

'It was after Maddy's funeral. She said everyone was on edge and she thought it best not to mention the toolbox find. Jon's reactions worried her, but then he'd just buried his daughter. She decided to wait and speak to me later.'

'When did she tell you all this?'

'This morning.'

'What did she do with the locket?'

'She has it with her. She wanted to show it to me; she's been online with a description of it and it links to a photo of a missing child.'

'Oh, God.' Zara breathed deeply.

Nathan looked directly at her. She noticed the dark shadows on his drawn face.

'It just gets worse, Nathan. Let's get you back to your room. Rest, and we'll talk later. And this evening, when Pippa's asleep, we need to tell Mum everything we know and suspect, even about Rachael O'Leary.'

Nathan nodded.

'How many more Rachaels do you think there are?' asked Zara with unease.

Nathan looked at Zara in anguish. 'I think Lisa's uncovered more than a box of jewellery. I think she's uncovered trophies. And not just from one girl.'

Zara walked Nathan back to the guest house, then went off in search of Izzy and Pippa. With his head lowered, Nathan stumbled gratefully towards his quarters, the thought of fresh linens and a cool mattress high on his agenda. He knew that shortly Martin Nesbitt would be calling for verification from the UK, and from then on, everyone would be sleeping less.

⌒

Leaving Pippa safely in the kitchen under Emily's watchful eye, Izzy and Lisa retired to the bedrooms for cool showers and to freshen up. Lisa had invited Izzy to use Maddy's room and there, after her shower, she lay down on the bed and closed her eyes, waiting for Zara to return from her talk with Nathan.

Gareth, engrossed in business calls in his bedroom, hadn't noticed or heard Jon's taxi arrive outside the Pink Villa. Neither had Lisa who, like Izzy, had showered and lay on the bed for a rest, wrapped in a fresh towel. Not even Zara, by now making her way through the main house towards Maddy's bedroom, heard or saw anything.

Jon entered the kitchen through the back door, dumped his small bag on the tiled floor, removed a small bottle and placed it carefully in his pocket. He'd already dressed for the sun and water, wearing deck shoes, shorts and a dark blue T-shirt. Striding towards Pippa, he swept her up into his arms, laughing as he did so.

'The *Phoenix*?' he asked, grinning at his beautiful daughter. 'You can play captain and steer the boat,' he told her.

'Can we go to the secret beach, Daddy? I know how to get there.'

'Wherever!' he replied.

Without a moment's hesitation, Pippa nodded, laughing excitedly at the prospect and throwing her arms tightly around his neck.

'I can cook a special meal for you tonight, Mr Stone,' Emily suggested, watching and listening to the scheming pair.

'No thank you, Emily,' said Jon with a grin. 'We won't be back for dinner.'

Pippa squealed in delight, 'Are we staying out all night, Daddy?'

'Not *all* night, but we'll be out until very late,' he said chuckling. Then, having collected the boat key from the hook on the kitchen wall, he waved Emily goodbye, throwing Pippa over his shoulder as they rushed out. It took moments for them to reach the end of the garden and then both disappeared from view. Emily, smiling, returned to her chores.

No one other than Emily knew Jon had arrived back at the villa. No one realised he'd gone off in the *Phoenix*. No one knew he'd taken Pippa with him.

Lisa nestled into her bed and opened her book. As the words swam, she closed her eyes and gently nodded off.

Zara entered her bedroom to find Gareth still engrossed in his business calls. Kissing him quietly on the cheek, she wandered off down the corridor in search of Izzy. Knocking on Maddy's door, she pushed it open. 'Thought you'd be in here.' She smiled. 'Are you ok?'

'I am, and thank you for inviting me here today. Maddy spoke of this villa with such love and affection. I can see why.'

Zara smiled. 'My pleasure. I'm sure if things had taken a different turn, Maddy would have brought you here herself.' Sad looks crossed both girls' faces. 'I've spoken to Nathan. He's having a lie down now. When he feels rested, we're going to speak to my mother. The best time would be after Pippa goes to bed.'

They both knew that what Lisa would discover tonight would probably send her into an emotional meltdown.

'I can look after Pippa if you feel you need to speak to her any earlier,' suggested Izzy, happy to remove herself from that meeting.

Zara sighed. 'I'm not looking forward to this either, Izzy,' she said, reading her mind. 'And no, thank you, we need you with us; it's going to be a difficult conversation, with lots of questions. I'm relying on both Nathan's and your support, with what I'm going to tell her.'

'Ok,' Izzy replied, shivering at the thought.

'Coffee?' asked Zara, a sense of chill spreading through her bones.

'Please!'

'Let's go out into the sunshine. I don't know about you, but I'm feeling cold in the air-conditioning.'

Izzy nodded. She too felt a chill, but she didn't believe it was from the air-conditioning alone.

'By the way,' Zara asked as they walked out of the bedroom. 'Is that picture on the wall one of yours?'

Izzy turned to where Zara pointed and smiled. 'Yes, I gave that to Maddy as a gift. It's of our secret beach.'

They walked together towards the deserted sun loungers and pool area. 'Stay here in the sun, Izzy. I'll go and get us some coffees,' said Zara, turning her head as Emily walked towards them with a pile of dry towels. 'Hi Emily, what have you done with Pippa?' she asked.

'Gone on the boat with Mr Stone.'

'Jon!' both girls cried in unison, the smiles on their faces instantly vanishing.

'Yes,' Emily answered with hesitation, aware of the tension and alarmed by their worried expressions. 'Did I do something wrong?' she asked, the pile of washing suddenly feeling heavy in her arms.

'No Emily, you did nothing wrong,' assured Zara. 'Please, when did they leave?'

Emily shrugged. She hadn't taken note of the time. 'I'm not sure. I emptied the dishwasher, did some potatoes for dinner and emptied the spin drier ... it must have been about forty minutes ago. He just left his bag in the kitchen and went with Pippa directly down to the *Phoenix*.'

'Did he say where they were going?' Zara's voice rose in fear as she spoke; she could also feel Maddy connecting to her strongly.

Emily shook her head, her dark eyes wide now with concern. 'Not to me, but I heard him tell Pippa she could steer. And there was something about a secret beach.'

'Ah,' murmured Izzy, catching Zara's eye.

'Pippa was very excited to go,' Emily said, defensively.

Zara nodded, patting her arm. 'We'll go find her, don't you worry.'

'The secret beach!' said Maddy, her voice loud in Zara's head, the connection now frighteningly powerful. 'Izzy knows where it is. It's very private, secluded, perfect place for Jon to … You must hurry. He knows I can't protect Pippa now.'

Zara looked at Izzy. 'Do you remember how to get to the secret beach?' she asked.

'Yes, but it's not called that. That's just the name we gave to the secluded stretch of sand.'

'What's the real name and can you get to it by car?' Zara asked.

'No, and I don't know its real name. I only know how to find it from the water.'

'Then we need a boat,' responded Zara, her face displaying all of Maddy's fears.

'Where's Jon's boat?' Izzy asked.

'Club Nautico! Palma marina. Too far,' Zara replied. 'And I couldn't use it, even if it was moored below, could you?'

Izzy shook her head. 'What about calling the Guardia Civil?' she suggested, her mind now filled with the terrible stories Maddy had confessed to her. 'Can't they help?'

Zara shook her head. 'They won't be interested, and what can we tell them? Jon is Pippa's father and entitled to take his daughter out sailing.'

'Mathew!' exclaimed Izzy, scrabbling for her phone. 'We need to call Mathew, get him to take us out there on his rib. It's very fast and if we hurry, we can catch them up.'

'What's all the fuss about?' asked Gareth, walking towards them. The girls shot a glance at one another as a wide-eyed Emily looked on.

'Jon's arrived early. He's taken Pippa out on the *Phoenix*.'

Zara watched the blood drain from Gareth's face, the thought of what could happen trickling down his spine like iced water. 'We need to stop him,' he said, without hesitation. 'We need a boat to chase him; someone must have one down below we can use?'

Zara shook her head. 'I think most of the neighbours keep their boats in the local marina. Maddy was the exception to the rule with the *Phoenix*. There are a number of dinghies for *cala*-crawling, but nothing I've seen that we could use to chase the *Phoenix*. I think there's a small sail boat down there, but none of us can sail and it doesn't look that seaworthy. And even if it was, it'd be far too slow to catch them up,' Zara said.

'No, wait!' exclaimed Izzy, her hand in the air. 'I've got Mathew here on the phone.' Gareth and Zara listened as Izzy explained the urgency while Emily, now sensing the seriousness of the situation, crumpled onto a sunbed, the precious laundry tumbling around her solid form.

'Mathew's en route to our *cala* now,' she told them. 'Hurry! By the time we get down to the beach, he'll be there to meet us. His crew are making the *Water Hawk* sea-ready as we speak.'

Gareth knew the vessel well, having always longed to sail on it. 'You two go down to the beach,' said Gareth. 'I'll drive down to the marina and join the *Water Hawk* from there. Tell Mathew I'll be there within the next twenty minutes.' Gareth knew that a high-performance rib could easily catch up with the *Phoenix*, which, even on motor sailing, couldn't do much more than eight to ten knots, depending on sea conditions. According to Izzy, Mathew's rib did at least forty knots. 'Jon can't have got too far. Once you guys spot it, the *Water Hawk* can then act as back-up.'

Zara knew Gareth's suggestion made sense; providing the *Phoenix* stayed in the immediate *cala* waters, they could pursue it in the rib, but if Jon tracked out to sea towards Ibiza, they would need a different vessel. God only knew what his intentions really were.

'What's happening?' asked a sleep-clouded Lisa, looking for Pippa and instead finding an anxious, huddled group around the pool. All faces turned to hers as she scanned their worried expressions. Stepping towards her, Zara took her mother's hand briefly. 'Mum, you need to go and wake Nathan. Tell him Jon's taken Pippa out on the *Phoenix* to the "secret beach". There's something he needs to tell you.'

'Jon's here already? I don't understand. What's happened?' she asked, looking at Emily who sobbed loudly. 'Where are you all going?' Lisa asked with concern

'To get Pippa,' answered Zara as calmly as she could with Maddy's voice in her head screaming at her to hurry.

Lisa's eyes darkened with fear, grabbing onto her daughter's arm. 'What is it you know that I don't?' Zara's eyes flickered with fright. 'Is Pippa safe?' Lisa asked.

'She will be,' assured Gareth. 'I need your car, Lisa. Where are the keys?'

'They should be under the sun visor. But what's happened?' she asked again in panic as all three began moving away from her.

'Speak to Nathan, Mum. Now!' The urgency in Zara's voice was frightening. 'We've got to go.'

Black thoughts whirled around Lisa's head as she watched Zara and Izzy run across the lawn towards the beach path. Unable to comprehend, but aware of the obvious tension, she tried to make sense of what was happening around her.

The terrified look Emily gave her chilled her to her very soul. Something was desperately wrong. With a small cry, she ran towards Nathan in the guest house.

Out on the villa's driveway, Gareth yanked open Lisa's car door. Leaping in, he pulled down the sun visor and waited for the keys to drop into his lap. *Good old Lisa,* he thought, turning the key in the ignition and tossing his mobile onto the passenger seat. Selecting a gear, he threw the car onto the dirt track and made his way down to the main road, heading for the local marina. Checking his watch, he knew he needed to hurry; Mathew may need the support of the *Water Hawk* out on the water.

Zara and Izzy negotiated the treacherous steps down to the beach like mountain goats, hearts in their mouths. They reached the small stretch of sand and, running across the bleached boards, short of breath, went out onto the jetty to where Mathew waited in the *Water Hawk*'s tender. As Izzy jumped in, Mathew started the engine. 'Cast off, Zara,' he told her. Zara untied the boat and nimbly leapt in as the small craft punched its way across the water. Zara held on tightly, the black and cream plastic seat covers warm to her back. Any other time, this ride would have been exhilarating, but today it felt terrifyingly dangerous.

There was no time to lose. Knowing what Jon was capable of, Mathew wasn't going to hang around. 'So, which way?' he asked, motoring out towards the open waters. Mathew glanced back at Izzy's windblown face. 'Left or right out of here?'

'Right, and hug the coastline. It's some way yet and the beach is tucked well back and easy to miss.'

'Don't worry, we'll see the *Phoenix* before she gets there. This boat can outrun her easily,' said Mathew, turning to look at Izzy's tightly controlled face.

God, I hope so! thought Izzy.

Zara sat in silence, Maddy's voice dripping words into her head.

'This is what I feared the most – that one day, he would initiate Pippa into the role I played as a child.'

Zara shuddered, and a small cry escaped her lips. 'We'll get there, Maddy,' she whispered. 'Don't worry. I'll keep Pippa safe. Just stay with me and tell me what to do.' Her words, carried away on the offshore breeze, were heard by only Maddy.

Chapter 29

Nathan had been dreaming. A disturbing dream in which he'd found Rachael O'Leary wandering down on the beach. She looked older than the image in the photo, her smile and face more beautiful to him. He was running to catch up with her, but the faster he ran, the farther away she appeared to be. Exhausted, he stopped running and, standing on the sand, he called out to her. She turned towards him, the wind playing with her long red hair; then, opening her arms, she called his name. A dull banging sound filled his head as he tried to answer her.

'Nathan!' Lisa cried, beating on the guest-house door.

Women's cries, both real and in his dreams, merged. Aware of Lisa's knocking, Nathan pulled himself from his restless slumber, left the rumpled bed and wrapped a bathrobe around his frail body before opening the door.

'Jon's back and he's taken Pippa out on the *Phoenix*. Everyone's rushed off to get Pippa,' Lisa spluttered, distraught. 'What's going on? What do I need to know, Nathan? Tell me, please!'

Nathan took Lisa's hands and guided her towards the unmade bed. 'Sit. Please sit,' he said. 'What I'm about to tell you will be difficult for you to hear.'

Nathan pulled up a chair, sat down in front of a trembling Lisa and began to tell his side of the story. As the terrible truth trickled out, Lisa dragged the bed linen around her, desperate to protect herself from the horrendous details. The more she learnt, the further she retreated into the covers, until finally, racked with pain, she rolled herself into a tight ball and sobbed. Nathan, himself exhausted with guilt and grief, leant back in his chair and cried the tears of a condemned man.

Chapter 30

They saw the *Phoenix* tucked into a cove ahead with her sails furled and sun awning up. Izzy had been right. The secret beach could only be reached by water, as even the surrounding land was too treacherous and steep to provide a pathway down. Tucked behind a jutting piece of rocky headland, the beach itself was little more than a ribbon of cream-coloured sand, not enough to tempt the passing locals or those with larger craft. The *Phoenix* lay anchored close to the mouth of the inlet; its tender bobbed in the water, attached to the stern.

As they approached, Zara could see inside the little boat, where two oars lay casually in the bottom. There was no outboard motor on the dinghy. The simple and cleverly designed white canvas sun awning had obviously been hurriedly erected – thrown over the boom and strapped down using its Velcro strips and cord straps to secure. Normally, this structure would be tied to the main mast, backstay and tails; today, it almost floated over the cockpit.

'Dangerous. One strong wind and the whole thing will lift and pull away. A whipping cord could put an eye out!' warned Maddy.

'Not our main concern, Maddy, but I hear you,' replied Zara, ducking to see under the awning as Mathew manoeuvred the rib alongside. 'No sign of them; they must be down below in the galley,' said Zara, hopefully.

'Or the cabin,' said Maddy, ominously.

Her heart thumping, Zara tied a rope to one of the *Phoenix*'s cleats as Mathew cut the engine. 'Hello there!' she shouted, trying to see inside the porthole windows. There was no reply. 'I'm going on,' she said.

Mathew helped her climb up onto the sailing boat, while Izzy, using the *Phoenix*'s rails, steadied the rib alongside. With no sails up and a calm sea, the *Phoenix* hardly rocked. Climbing nimbly up onto the deck, Zara took the bowline from Mathew and tied the rubber rib firmly before making her way towards the covered helm.

Although the *Phoenix* was fitted with all the most up-to-date automated devices, Jon hadn't bothered with any sails during his journey to the secret beach, preferring to rely on the engine for motoring, allowing Pippa to play 'Captain' at the helm. Zara looked up at the carefully packed canvas bags strad-dling the masts and boom like fat caterpillars. As she padded the teak deck towards the covered cockpit, she listened. There was no sound from below.

'We may be too late,' Maddy told her, her sense of panic and fear seeping through Zara's body.

'God, I hope not. Hello there!' Zara shouted again.

The sounds of feet above deck woke Jon in his cabin. Lifting himself up on one elbow, he waited and listened.

'Hello … anyone on board? Pippa?' Zara called.

'Damn!' Jon muttered, recognising the voice as he wrapped and tied his short sarong around his waist. Lisa hated the wraps he wore in the sun, banning him from wearing them in polite company. 'They don't leave much to the imagination,' she would point out. Today, Jon wanted what he shouldn't show to be on display; today was a special day for him: no Lisa, just his daughter, Pippa. He'd even wrapped up a charm for her as a gift to mark this particular day – a silver heart that opened to reveal another, inside of which sat a tiny gold one. A unique gift for a special girl. 'Zara. Damn!' he mumbled again, heading out of the master cabin into the galley. As he reached the steps up into the cockpit and looked up, he saw Zara's face peering down.

On finding the *Phoenix*, Mathew had used his VHF to contact the *Water Hawk*, standing them down from the chase and asking that Gareth ensure Nathan and Lisa knew. The relieved crew dropped anchor and took some time out to enjoy the flat sea and cloudless skies.

For Izzy, both tearful and reassured, the return to the secret beach and the presence of the *Phoenix* hurt. Still mourning for Maddy, she suddenly found herself unable to contain her emotions. This particular piece of coastline held haunting memories. It was here that she and Maddy had spent time together, the sand between their toes, the sun on their bodies, their hearts filled with love, playing in and out of the waves. Both strong swimmers, the stretch of water between the *Phoenix* and the beach held no danger for them and they'd dive off the boat like a couple of wild dolphins. That's why she and Maddy had chosen the dolphin rings – a symbol of their love, emotional and physical, eternally entwined. Twisting her own ring on her finger, she made a decision: she'd have to swim out to the beach. Understanding her pain and assured of her safety, Mathew watched her dive off the rib into the water, swimming soundlessly towards the beach. He realised the difficulties Izzy faced, knowing all that she knew, and that being in close proximity to Jon would be impossible for her. Turning away, Mathew took in a deep breath before climbing up onto the deck of the *Phoenix*. Whatever happened next, he knew Izzy would be best off in the water or on the beach.

On board the *Phoenix*, Jon's heart didn't miss a beat. He climbed smoothly up the galley steps and onto the deck, just as Mathew joined Zara, ducking under the low canvas awning. They watched Jon's eyes as he smiled warmly. 'Sorry, just having forty winks, so peaceful here,' he told them, stretching out his hand towards Mathew in a polite greeting. 'Have we met?' he asked.

'No,' Mathew replied, shaking Jon's hand, a buzz of uncomfortable energy passing between them. 'My name's Mathew. I'm a friend of … Zara's.' Something made him wary of mentioning Izzy.

'Welcome aboard,' replied Jon with an accommodating grin, waving his hands in a circular motion as if the boat belonged to him.

'My boat!' said Maddy, watching her father through Zara's eyes. 'Not his. And he hasn't strapped that awning down properly,' she remarked again.

Zara looked up at the awning above.

'Such a beautiful day. I came back early and thought I'd surprise Pippa and rush her out to watch the sun go down this evening on the *Phoenix*. Maddy would have liked that. I knew you couldn't sail the *Phoenix* by yourself, and as the sea looked so flat I decided to just go for it. Impulsive, I know, but Pippa was up for it. Hope you're not here because I took the boat unannounced?' he laughed. 'Didn't have time to tell Lisa, although I knew Emily would, and now my mobile's flat!' Jon had ignored several calls and messages from Lisa and Nathan. His phone, fully charged, lay switched off, discarded in a drawer in the master cabin. 'Anyhow, we can't fall out over things like the ownership of boats and villas, can we? We must consider Pippa's happiness.'

Maddy cringed within Zara's body, her anger building by the minute.

Zara felt Jon's view of happiness for Pippa fell short of ok or even acceptable. But she smiled politely, willing Maddy to calm down. 'We did wonder where the boat had gone,' lied Zara. 'Mum had no idea you were even coming back, let alone intending to take the *Phoenix* out to sea with Pippa.'

'As I said, impulse, Zara. I missed my Pippa, and the idea just came to me as I drove up to the villa.'

'Where is Pippa?' Zara asked, spotting a small red swimsuit pegged onto a rail, as she looked around for evidence of her little sister.

'Sleeping. She's exhausted herself with all that swimming. Can't believe the *liveliness* of that child. Unstoppable!'

Zara felt Maddy rise within her, her own body trembling at those words.

Maddy remembered. Remembered the 'chasing game' in the pool, when he'd encourage her to exhaust herself, swimming until she was physically unable to do any more, drained, unable to fight, the taste of chlorine in her mouth and nose, the fear of drowning. Then he'd take advantage; his fingers hurting her softer regions, the rough concrete of the poolside scraping her tender skin. 'Bastard!' she screamed.

'I'll go down now and wake her,' Jon continued as Zara gathered her senses, her heart pumping fast with fear and anger.

'I'm sure she'd like something to eat, and we were going to take the tender off around the next point to find a tapas beach restaurant. Pippa wanted an ice cream. Perhaps you'd both like to join us?' His smile was open and friendly.

Take the 'tender' without a motor? *thought Maddy.*

Ignoring Jon, Zara tucked her head below deck and called out. The wind caught Jon's sarong, displaying parts of his body Zara preferred not to see. 'It's all right, Jon, I'll get her,' said Zara, squeezing past him with a shudder. She ducked down into the cabin, her heart in her mouth.

Holding his breath, Mathew waited until he could hear Zara's voice and the excited gabble of a small child. Relieved, he asked, 'So what restaurant were you thinking of? Not much around here.' He took a seat on the cushioned bench inside the cockpit and, resting his elbows on the teak table in front, he continued, 'The closest beach bar is some way off around the next head and I noticed you don't have the outboard engine on the dinghy.'

Jon's eyes narrowed in thought, his earlier lie a slip. 'Did I say tender? I intended to up anchor and motor the *Phoenix* there,' he hastily glossed.

'My rib would be the fastest to get us all there,' suggested Mathew, worried now by the lateness of the day. He wanted to get Pippa and Zara as far away from Jon as he could.

Jon nodded, peering through the lines and over the side to where Mathew's black rib lay. 'Impressive vessel. How fast does it go?' he asked.

'Forty knots,' Mathew said, his bright blue eyes momentarily sparkling with pride.

'How many can she seat?'

'Six, comfortably.'

'Life vests?'

'Obviously. But I'd suggest you bring Pippa's. I don't have anything that small on board,' Mathew replied, feeling uncomfortable with Jon's pleasantness. Even his welcoming smile earlier had appeared genuine. The sound of laughter interrupted them as a naked Pippa emerged through the cabin door, her salt-drenched hair sticking out in all directions. 'Where's my costume?' she asked. Then seeing Mathew, she darted back below, into the arms of a laughing Zara, who wrapped her in a towel before propelling her up on deck.

'Hello, Pippa,' said Mathew. 'I'm a friend of Zara's. If you're looking for your swimsuit, that one looks like yours,' he told her, pointing to the tiny red garment pegged to the railings.

'It's been drying in the sun,' said Jon, carefully unpegging it and passing it down to her.

'Ooh, thank you. It's dry now,' replied Pippa, and discarding the towel and her modesty, she pulled on her bathing costume before asking her father for a drink.

Jon smiled, looking around at his guests. 'I think we could all do with one, don't you?' he said, climbing down into the galley as he called back. 'I've found several bottles of good Champagne down here too.'

'Mine!' hissed Maddy. 'Stored for our celebrations after the getaway.'

Zara cringed, hearing and sensing the pain in Maddy's words. She joined Pippa on the cushioned bench, opposite Mathew. With Pippa huddled on her lap, she mouthed the word *safe* to Mathew, folding her arms protectively around her sister's tiny frame.

Pippa twisted on her bottom and lifted her face towards Zara's, her bright eyes wide with excitement. 'I'm glad you're here with us; Daddy said today was going to be the most important day of my life. Now you can share it too.'

'Bastard!' screamed Maddy.

Unaware of the reaction she'd caused, Pippa slid off Zara's lap, calling down to her father for crisps. Zara turned towards Mathew, shocked. His expression warned her to keep her emotions in check – a near-impossible feat with all she'd learnt recently and Maddy's constant input.

Where's Izzy? she mouthed.

'On the beach,' he told her quietly. 'She's hurting and very worried.'

Zara leant out and looked over the side, but she couldn't

see anything from the boat. She shook her head and thought, *Perhaps it's best she's not on board at this moment in time. I'm not sure I could cope with both girls in my head.*

'Nearly there,' whispered Mathew. 'Stay strong. We have Pippa now.'

Zara nodded. *Not safe yet, but at least we're all here with her,* she thought, dropping her defences in relief.

'Keep alert, Zara. My father can't be trusted,' warned Maddy.

Jon knew his plans for Pippa would now need to be changed. Mentally checking his options, he made the decision to play along with the beach-bar suggestion, serving his uninvited guests a couple of Champagne cocktails first. He'd brought along a small bottle of his faithful 'elixir' for emergencies; he knew that would guarantee a deep sleep in the sun. Perhaps his plans for Pippa would not be totally ruined. And anyway, the risk factor always heightened his excitement and enhanced his performance. Pippa would easily play the game if she thought Zara was in danger. A few carefully chosen words would do it; they always did. Their 'little secret' would be safe. She'd never risk losing Zara as well as Maddy. As for Mathew, well, he'd wait until the Rohypnol took effect and then tip him back into his rib and cut him loose. There would be no danger of discovery. Zara would stay on the boat in one of the cabins and return with them, none the wiser, to the Pink Villa. As far as those back at the villa were concerned, they would all have had a lovely afternoon out on the boat. Zara would have had too much to drink and passed out, and the explanation for Mathew would be that he must have taken himself off on his rib for a drunken kip and suffered a nasty case of sunburn. All in all, an easy explanation. Only Pippa would know the truth; and Jon knew from experience how best to manage that situation. Child's play for someone in his profession. Any sullenness or noticeable changes in Pippa's personality after today, would be easily explained as delayed psychological shock and grief at Maddy's passing. All blamed on the trip back to the secret beach and the opening up of supressed emotional memories. Jon chuckled. After today's 'initiation', he'd live with the memory of it for a while. He'd use Lisa's body for a little longer, then, with some careful medicating, he'd ensure she slept soundly at night, like Tilly always did, leaving him free to pick up where he'd left off with Pippa. His only concern was Lisa's discovery of the toolbox and his personal spoils. That was unfortunate. His own clumsy mistake – he'd never expected her to go rummaging in his old shed; she'd always been so grateful for his love and therefore overly trusting and unsuspecting. Her finding the toolbox and his trophies and the subsequent questions were therefore out of character. He'd since removed those articles and carefully hidden them; but he had every intention of adding to these 'spoils' at a later date.

As Jon carefully measured and mixed his cocktails, dripping the contents of his precious bottle into two plastic Champagne flutes, he hummed to himself. *Supposed to be for emergencies,* he thought. *But then, this is just that – isn't it?*

Pippa sat on Zara's lap clutching a feast-sized crisp packet. She crammed one hand into the greasy foil packet, grabbed a fistful of crisps and stuffed them into her tiny mouth.

'Hungry?' Zara asked with a grin.

Pippa nodded, the rhythm of the 'crisp dive' undisturbed.

Mathew smiled as he watched Zara try to finger-comb Pippa's salt-starched hair. 'Not sure where the most salt is, in your hair or on your hands now?' she muttered, planting a kiss on one of Pippa's warm shoulders.

Pippa chuckled, a fine spray of munched crisps escaping her lips.

'Sorry I took so long,' said Jon, returning from the galley with the two plastic Champagne glasses and a bottle tucked under one arm. 'Champagne cocktails for the grown-ups, it's a kir royale of sorts,' he explained, passing the sparkling liquid to both Zara and Mathew before diving back down for his own glass and water for Pippa. 'Here's to a memorable sundown,' he toasted on his return, settling beside Mathew. 'And here's to our dear Maddy. May she be looking down on us all today!' he added with a smile.

Zara lifted the plastic flute with the bubbling liquid to her mouth. 'To Maddy,' she replied, *who's closer than you know*, she thought. Sipping gently, she allowed the fizz to bounce off her parched tongue, wishing she'd drunk more water before she left the villa. The smooth cocktail was easy to swallow and tasted good.

'No, Zara,' warned Maddy as the first trickle slipped down Zara's parched throat. 'Toss it! I don't trust him; he could have put something in it.'

Unsure, Zara paused momentarily as Mathew raised his glass and drank deeply.

'Zara! He's not inviting you to drink for social reasons. Be careful,' Maddy warned.

'Here, Mathew. You must have been thirsty. Let me top you up,' said Jon pouring more Champagne into his flute and beckoning Pippa away from Zara for a small taste of his own drink.

Zara smiled politely as she surreptitiously tipped her own Champagne onto the abandoned towel lying close to her on the cushions, the parched fibres silently absorbing the liquid.

'*You need to stop Mathew from drinking any more,*' cautioned *Maddy.*

'Let me top you up too,' Jon told Zara, as Mathew's shoulders relaxed and he leant back in his seat, his eyelids starting to droop.

'*Too late, Zara. He's emptied his glass. Don't you have any more.*'

Zara shook her head. 'No thanks, I'm fine,' she answered, beginning to sink back against the damp towel, the small amount she'd swallowed already spreading through her body, taking the edge off her senses. As she lay back in the sunshine, all tension in her shoulders began to unravel.

'*Zara!*' shrieked *Maddy.*

Closing her eyes for a moment, Zara allowed herself the brief luxury of nothingness as the boat gently rocked.

'*Zara!*' *Maddy screamed again within her head.*

Zara heard the internal screaming, her survival instincts aroused.

'*Zara, wake up. I hope you're faking? If not, we are in serious trouble.*'

Through half-closed eyelids, Zara watched Jon move towards Pippa, his arms outstretched.

'*Zara!*' *Maddy shouted.*

Chapter 31

With both Zara and Mathew asleep on deck, Jon was back in control. 'It looks like Mathew and Zara are going to take a snooze up here,' he told Pippa. 'Perhaps we should leave them for a bit? I've found some of your favourite fizzy orange in the galley fridge. Shall we go down and get some to wash down those crisps?'

'Yes please,' Pippa answered, standing up from her seated position behind the cockpit table and carefully traversing the length of the cushioned bench so as not to disturb anyone. Jon smiled, lowering himself down the cabin steps as Pippa raced ahead of him.

'Wake up, Zara,' Maddy *screamed from within Zara's inert body, now slumped back into the cushions. 'How much did you drink?'*

'I hear you, Maddy, but my body isn't behaving as it should,' Zara answered, squinting towards the galley opening where a smiling Jon stood watching her.

'Hello, pretty Zara,' he whispered. 'Pity, but my tastes are for sweeter flesh, so you can sleep on. If I change my mind, I know where I can find you.'

Zara watched Jon disappear down into the cabin as Maddy squirmed inside her. *'You have to get help and stop him, Zara. Where's Izzy?'*

'I don't know. Mathew said she went to the beach some time back.'

'Try and attract her attention if you can. She needs to get help over here – and fast.'

Zara looked around her. Mathew lay unconscious opposite her and she couldn't see anything else from her position on the bench.

'Well, we are on our own now, girl. If you had doubts before as to Jon's intentions, I'm sure you don't now.'

'Oh, God. What do I do?' Zara asked, glancing over in Mathew's direction. 'Everything seems slightly off-kilter, Maddy. How do I wake him?'

'You can't, so he won't be much help. You need to get up, find a phone and get the Water Hawk *over here fast. Or use the radio and call for help. Tell them Mathew's collapsed on board.'*

'Why can't I just shout for Jon? Tell him that Mathew's out cold and I'm worried – tell him we need to get help?'

Maddy's frustration almost burst through Zara's body. 'He won't help you. He's the one that drugged him in the first place; you were also supposed to go to sleep. Do you really think he'd help either of you now? He's got more important things on his mind than your welfare. My father doesn't like interference or mess.'

Maddy's words frightened Zara. 'I hear you, Maddy. But I've already told you – my brain and limbs don't seem to be coordinating.'

'Christ! What was it he put in your drink?'

'I only had a slurp.'

The sound of a frightened child, calling out in panic, the pitch raised, drilled deep within Zara.

'Nooo …!' Pippa screamed.

Shocked by the fear in Pippa's voice, Zara's sluggish body responded, her stomach tightening and her heart thumping as the adrenaline pumped through her veins, counteracting the effects of the drug.

'MOVE. NOW!' screamed Maddy as both girls, one living, one dead, combined their strength to fuse as one.

Now able to move, anger coursing through her body, Zara climbed down into the galley where she could see Pippa's small, inert body lying on one of the guest-cabin beds. There was no sign of Jon as she crept along the carpeted galley floor. Pippa was lying on her back, her face pale and her eyes closed. Zara checked for a pulse. She was breathing but obviously unconscious, a thin trickle of blood on her right temple.

Maddy squirmed in fury as Zara surveyed the scene.

The sound of a flush from the heads in the bow alerted Zara.

'Move her, Zara,' instructed Maddy.

Gently collecting Pippa into her arms, Zara braced herself.

'Up top. You'll need to get her off the Phoenix. Use Mathew's rib. Just get her in it and I'll help you start it.'

Shaking with fear and adrenaline, Zara scurried back up onto the deck just as Jon opened the toilet door. Standing in the cockpit, with Pippa trailing in her arms, Zara heard a noise above her as Jon snapped the flimsy straps on one side of the awning to expose them. Looking up, she gasped. She could see him clearly now on the cabin roof, his sarong tucked around his loins, a small anchor in his hands, an open hatch behind him.

'Shit!' murmured Maddy. 'Not good.'

Zara shivered. The anchor, sharp and folded flat, was lightweight and portable. Maddy had stored it in a locker in the galley, wrapped in a towel, to be used as a secondary anchoring device in shallow waters. Today, in Jon's hands, it became a potentially lethal instrument.

'You are a fool, Zara,' Jon told her. 'This trip was supposed to be Pippa's initiation. Now you have ... complicated things.'

'I know what you did to Maddy!' she shouted, hoping Izzy was within earshot or that Mathew would wake. 'I also know that Pippa's not only Maddy's child, but yours too. You are her father … and her grandfather.'

Jon's eyes narrowed as he listened to Zara. 'You shouldn't have got involved, Zara,' he said, inching towards her. 'My game, my rules. Maddy knew that.'

Zara's eyes never left his large, tanned hands, holding the anchor like a weapon.

'She tried to change the game plan too.'

Zara stepped back, towards the stern, her precious cargo held tightly. 'Is that what Maddy did to you? Tried to change things, threatened to expose your sickening activities? Is that why you killed her?'

Jon's face registered the accusation from his lofty position above the cockpit entrance.

'She was a fool … thought she could take Pippa away from me. I will not be played, Zara. Maddy tried to play me. Only I was two steps ahead; the rules are mine to make … She knew the terms.'

'What terms? To keep quiet about your abuse, in order to protect Pippa?' shouted Zara, her face now streaked with her own tears, desperate for Mathew to wake or Izzy to help her. 'She didn't even know for sure that Pippa was her own daughter until recently, did she? You even took that from her,' sobbed Zara, hugging Pippa close. Did you know she asked Nathan where her baby boy was buried?'

Jon paused. 'So Nathan has become my loose link! And I suppose *he* knows too?' he said, glancing over at Mathew's crumpled body on the bench, partially hidden now by one side of the awning. 'Pity he won't be around for much longer to support your allegations. I have a tidy plan for you both now.'

Stalling, Zara continued, desperate for some sort of instruction from Maddy and still hoping someone would come to her aid. 'You used Pippa to keep Maddy in check, didn't you? She must have been terrified that you might do to Pippa what you did to her. Why, Jon? Why?'

Jon transferred the anchor to his other hand and looked straight at Zara. 'From my loins … therefore, mine to do with as I please.'

'No, Jon. Not yours to do with as you please!' screamed Zara. 'Maddy was your daughter and should have received the love and protection of a father, not your warped sexual advances. She died trying to prove the truth and protect Pippa.'

Jon remained where he was, looking down on an incensed and frightened Zara. 'You really don't understand, do you? I loved Maddy. I had plans for her; and Pippa. We were going to live together, in the Pink Villa, just us, the perfect family. Incest is not a crime here in Majorca. Direct bloodlines, over the age of consent, living as a couple are acceptable. So too any children resulting from their relationship. Pippa could have been legitimately ours here.'

'Never!' screamed Maddy.

'But you're not a Spanish citizen. You're English and incest is a crime,' argued Zara.

'It's the country that determines the law, Zara, and incest was removed as a crime in the Spanish Constitution. Maddy knew this. I told her so.'

'But it is still a crime when below the age of consent,' argued Maddy. 'I told him that! My father wanted me to agree to his plans, live here on my inheritance.'

'No, Jon. Maddy was a child when she got pregnant, under the age legally in both countries. That's paedophilia and incest.'

Jon smiled slowly. 'No longer an issue,' he replied, shrugging his shoulders. 'Maddy's gone, and those may be the facts, but in making them known Pippa gets damaged. You won't do that. I know; Maddy didn't want the truth to come out either. A little squeamish about Daddy being the father of her own daughter.'

The sickening confession and veiled threats shocked Zara. 'And what about your wife? My mother … Lisa?'

'Ah,' sighed Jon, 'your mother? She was a necessary pawn in my game. I made her a "queen" for a few games, but she really couldn't hold up against my girls. Too old and fleshy for my tastes.'

Zara squirmed in disgust. 'So what did you intend to do with her?'

'Simple. Divorce her.' He laughed, standing upright against the blue sky, his face filled with delight. 'The properties belong to the Erskine Trust, so she can't touch those, and Pippa? Well, Pippa was never legally adopted. Mine by virtue of bloodline. All quite tidy … officially.'

'And now? What about me? How are you going to stop me and Mathew from going to the police?'

Jon chuckled. 'The police out here?' he smiled. 'On what charge? Speculation? Just for the record, nothing happened with me and Pippa; well, not much, anyway. She panicked and tried to get out of the cabin porthole window. I went to stop her and she hit her head on the catch. At worst, she'll have a bump when she wakes up. A simple case of mild concussion, not life-threatening. And as for Maddy's death? That's listed out here as an accident. No, I'm not worried about the police. Anyway, you won't get the chance to speak to them. Yours and Mathew's deaths will go down as a boating accident. The sea can be quite dangerous for those who drink too much on board; all too easy to hit one's head on metal objects, like the porthole catch that caught poor Pippa. Or this one!' Jon inclined his head towards the anchor. Then, walking towards

189

Zara, he lifted his weapon to shoulder height. 'Now I've wasted too much time talking. Pippa and I have some unfinished business to attend to before it gets dark and then I want to go back to my bed at the villa.'

'Wait!' shrieked Zara as Jon's shadow fell over her. 'You'll hurt Pippa.'

'Collateral damage. She'll be more amenable afterwards. Interesting what a little pain can do to the mind. Quite persuasive ...'

Zara moved, her brain searching for an escape.

Jon held his weapon tightly. 'Let's play, shall we?'

Chapter 32

J on moved towards Zara as she crept backwards, tucking herself behind the wheel, Pippa pressed tightly to her hammering heart.

Inside of Zara, Maddy watched her father, screaming out at him with fear and frustration, remembering all those moments when he'd hurt her, done things to her that nobody should, the nights he'd crept into her room and woken her, one hand firmly over her mouth to ensure her silence. Images and memories so graphic and sickening; scenes that would terrify an adult, let alone a child, all now playing out in Zara's head.

'No, Maddy, stop!' Zara begged, the intensity of the images overwhelming her and bringing with them a pain so severe she thought her head would explode. Sliding to the deck, she crumpled, one hand grasping the base of the helm, Pippa's body draped over her knees and her fear building as she watched Jon inch ever closer. 'Maddy,' she implored, 'stop doing what you're doing to me. I can't cope with the pain.'

Maddy felt angered beyond belief. Her psychic abilities growing by the moment, she tapped into Zara's mind, filling her head with still more unpleasant memories and draining her energy. 'I'd rather see you jump into the ocean and drown Pippa. That would be better than what he intends for her. Don't – I beg you – let my father touch her ... are you listening, Zara?'

'No, Maddy. I won't drown your daughter. Pippa needs to live. If you want to help her, you need to *get out* of me now. He's going to kill me and do whatever he wants to her. Help me now or leave me alone. Your anger is draining my strength.

I can't fight Jon and protect Pippa like this,' pleaded Zara, kissing the child's cradled head. 'Help us!' she sobbed.

'Give her up, Zara ...' Jon sang, still edging towards her. 'Nobody's here to help you.' Raising the anchor above his head he smiled. 'Such a pity Pippa's mother isn't here to protect her now.'

At that moment, there was a crash of thunder so loud that Jon, his weapon raised high, paused to look up at the rapidly darkening sky. Although it was well known that Majorcan summer storms could suddenly form, this one came instantly and from nowhere. Thick black clouds pulled a sinister veil across the face of the sun, extinguishing the light and bringing with them a wind and stinging rain that rocked the masts and pummelled the sea into a bubbling froth. Jon, unbalanced, struggled for a hold.

Zara looked about her. She had known the moment Maddy had left her body. It felt as if someone had pulled an imaginary plug and half her body weight had been forcibly expelled. Holding tightly to the wheel, she watched in disbelief as a faint, wispy image of Maddy energised above them, growing in shape and matter, silhouetted against the dark grey sky.

Ah, the smell of teak and the salt. How I've missed that, *thought Maddy as she hovered, looking down on a soaked Zara, Pippa huddled to her breast, cowering in fear on the cockpit deck. She saw too the momentary confusion in Jon's eyes and then the steely determination as he looked towards Zara. 'Oh no you don't,' she cried, gliding towards him. 'Now you'll see what a mother will do to protect her child.'*

Zara remained huddled on the cockpit deck, her body protecting Pippa's from the torrent of rain while searching for a position of safety, as the boat caught in the squall dipped and fought against its anchor chain, banging and pulling against the invisible force.

'Maddy, help us,' Zara cried out in terror as the boat violently rocked in the wind.

Maddy, now free of all confines, floated towards them. Hovering above Pippa, she gently blew on her small daughter's facial injury, the hatred towards her father intensifying. Lifting her face to the wet sky, she cried out – a tormented lament for all the ills perpetrated by Jon, her cry shriller than those of the screeching seagulls, swooping below the darkened skies in search of cover.

Hearing the unnatural sound, Jon paused, looking out beyond the hammering rain, seeing nothing but the anomalous blending of angry sea and sky.

'I see you ...' Maddy's voice whispered close to his ear. 'The power of a mother's love knows no bounds.'

Jon, the sharp anchor still in his hands, moved purposefully through the wind and driving rain.

Zara felt the boat tipping from side to side, the wind catching the flapping awning, tearing at its Velcro bindings, loosening the remaining ties as it beat frantically in the wind. Squinting into the rain, she looked up, registering the desperate movement of the tiny flag on top of the mast.

As if sensing the building tension on the boat, the sea had changed from grey to a deep black-blue. Soaked, cold and terrified, Zara could only watch as Jon approached her. Mathew, still unconscious, lay in a heap on the deck, unaware of what was unfolding around him. 'Maddy!' screamed Zara again, looking desperately around her. 'Where are you now that I need you?' she shouted into the wind. 'If you've stepped back into me, then help, you're the sailor ... I'm just your vessel! Steer me, Maddy.'

With the pitching of the boat Jon grasped the boat's slippery rail, the anchor in his hand scraping its metal. 'Stupid bitch!' he shouted into the wind. 'Why did you have to get involved? This was supposed to be a happy day for Pippa and me. Now you've ruined it. You'll all have to go.'

'Oh, God!' Zara's hands were now clumsy and shaking. She shuffled further back into the dipping stern, still clasping Pippa close to her. With one eye still on Jon, she viewed the rising sea and felt sick with fear. The dragging tender had flipped in the wind, its oars long gone.

He's going to hit us and push us overboard and no one will know the truth, thought Zara. 'Maddy, where are you?' she screamed into the wind.

'Shh … I'm here,' a voice whispered in her ear. 'I'm not leaving you …'

'Thank God. Tell me what to do,' said Zara, and as she twisted her face towards the voice she saw a clear image of Maddy.

'I can see you,' Zara cried.

'I know …'

'Can Jon?'

Maddy appeared to float a few inches off the deck as she surveyed the scene in front of her. *'I don't think so.'*

'What are you going to do?

'Watch.'

Zara was balanced precariously on the deck, Pippa's inert body now growing painfully heavy in her arms. 'Hurry, Maddy,' she whimpered as Jon crept closer to her. 'I can't go any further. I've run out of deck. There's nowhere to run.' Zara's voice held pure terror. 'Please … do something!'

A flash of forked lightning split the sky, illuminating a terrified Zara with the still unconscious Pippa draped in her arms. And it was then that Jon saw something other than his intended quarry, watching him from the mast above them. The image appeared and then disappeared with the lightning flash. Blinking against the rain, he looked again. The vision reappeared.

Stupefied, Jon watched the apparition draw closer, his reasoning mind refusing to believe his own eyes. Maddy swiped the air above him and he stumbled, losing his footing as he tripped on some unseen object. Crashing onto the rolling deck, his arms were splayed in panic, and as his face touched the teak, the anchor flew from his hands. Temporarily winded, Jon looked up in disbelief. 'No! You're not real!' he shouted to the mast, twisting around in the stinging rain as he searched for his ghostly opponent.

'Oh, but I am. Look!' called Maddy.

Directly above them more lightning criss-crossed the darkened skies like a cat's cradle. As Jon's eyes adjusted to the light show, he saw her again, hovering protectively above Zara and Pippa. 'You're dead!' Jon shouted to the apparition. 'You can't hurt me.'

'I dare you to come a step closer,' Maddy warned, swooping down and touching his face, as Jon, disoriented and disbelieving, clawed the empty air. 'Retribution,' she hissed. 'Now it's your turn to feel the constraints of fear, knowing you can't do a thing to stop it. Powerless. It's not a pleasant feeling, is it, Father? Knowing that someone is going to do something to you … and you can't prevent it.'

'You're not real,' spat Jon again, desperately looking around for an escape route. Zara watched as now, back on his feet, he took another step towards them, his gait clumsy, his weapon lost, but his intentions still terrifyingly clear.

'No!' shouted Zara, placing Pippa gently on the deck and standing between Jon and the child. Soaked and petrified, she took a half step back, now straddling Pippa.

'Move, bitch!' he commanded, his voice cold and threatening. 'She's mine.'

Lifting her face in defiance, Zara prayed for help as Jon's fist connected with her jaw. The force of the punch rattled her teeth, throwing her to the deck. Stepping over Zara's crumpled body, Jon reached out for Pippa as Zara, still reeling from the blow, stretched out her arms to shield her.

'Never!' the sound of Maddy's voice cut above the wind, and both looked up at the apparition gliding towards them.

'Maddy,' moaned Zara, her ears still ringing from Jon's punch.

Jon stared. Even as he faced this image of his dead daughter, his mind would not – could not – comprehend fully what he saw, nor her intentions. He laughed, an act of bravado. 'Won't be long, Maddy,' he taunted, his eyes filling with a mixture of hatred and barely disguised fear as the apparition floated closer. 'I've got some family here that are longing to join you.'

Just then, with an audible crack, the boom broke free, launching the loose canvas awning into the air. Jon stared at the material pirouetting and spinning above him, dancing in the wind, its cords wildly lashing his upturned face. He turned sideways, only to be hit by the corner of the canvas, a metal eyelet slashing him across his left eye, the force knocking him to his knees. Then, as the boat tipped to one side, he pitched forwards. His forehead took most of the force, caught on the edge of the cockpit ridge, his tanned skin splitting as he stumbled for a hold on the wet surface. Half blind from the eyelet flaying, he wiped away the blood with his wet arms and hands. Then, looking up, he saw the floating image of Maddy, magnificently terrifying in all her spectral glory.

With a surge of madness, Jon threw himself at the apparition as the storm finally released the remaining awning leash, funnelling the canvas towards him like a missile. Zara watched as Jon grappled with the twisting, wet canvas, the material wrapping itself around him like a shroud. He panicked in his half-blind state, staggering directly into the path of the swinging boom. The sickening sound of metal connecting with flesh and bone could be heard above the noise of the storm. Zara shuddered as Jon, partially wrapped in sailcloth, fell sideways, tipping off the edge of the *Phoenix* and into the water, the sodden awning and seawater finally swallowing him.

At the exact moment Jon sank into the water, the mysterious storm dispersed. The wind dropped as suddenly as it had started and, with that, the sea began to calm, lessening the pulling and banging of the anchor chain. There had been moments during the storm when Zara thought the *Phoenix* would break free of her anchorage and drag out to sea, but now, as the water settled, so too did the pitching and rolling of the boat. Looking up to the skies, Zara saw a milky sun break through the evaporating clouds, bright and constant, bringing with it the blue of the late-afternoon sky. Even the colour of the churning sea changed before her eyes, as currents of bright, sun-warmed water turned the ink-black to a soft green. There was a surreal calm. As the boat rocked gently, the rainwater evaporating from the teak deck, Zara held Pippa tightly, drinking in the welcome warmth, while crying with relief. 'Thank you, thank you,' she sobbed, over and over again.

Despite its extraordinary violence, the sea tornado had done little damage. Mathew's black rubber rib, part-filled with water, still clung tightly to the side of the boat, while the *Phoenix's* dinghy, tethered off the stern, had flipped over, its lines now wrapped around the swim ladder.

Steeling herself, Zara peered over the side. There was no sign of either the awning or Jon.

From the stretch of coastland overlooking the secret beach, and on other boats in the vicinity, people had seen and watched how the strange tornado-like weather anomaly had attached itself to a sailing boat. They'd witnessed the force of the storm from afar, but seen nothing of the drama that had taken place on board.

Zara could now hear the radio. Voices were calling out in Spanish and then English; a Mayday had been raised, she realised. Shell-shocked, she remained on the sodden deck, her breath still coming in short, hysterical gasps. Pippa lay safe on the cockpit bench and Mathew, still unconscious and now thoroughly drenched, was under the cockpit table. Both were oblivious to what had taken place.

'Zara, I have to leave now.' Maddy's voice was soft and gentle.

'Please don't. You can't go,' sobbed Zara, wet, frightened and emotionally spent as she looked at the pale image in front of her. 'What happens now?'

'You get on with your life. Jon's gone. Pippa's safe.'

'But what about the truth, Maddy? What do I tell people?'

'Whatever you need to tell them. The real truth doesn't matter to me any more. My father's dead. You and Pippa are no longer in danger. No one else will suffer as I did. Justice has been served. I can go now, knowing Pippa is in good hands. Look after her for me. Love her as your own. The rest is up to you. You must decide what needs to be told; but some things are best left unexplained. And that goes for my intervention too.'

'Will I see you again?' Zara asked, her mind still trying to comprehend all she'd experienced and survived.

'If you choose to look, you'll find me. Not as you see me now, but you'll be reminded of me, always. Listen with your heart, Zara …

your heart will know when I'm around. Always and forever, my darling. Always and forever.'

'Please don't leave me. I'm not ready for you to go.' Zara wept, looking in Pippa's direction.

'I have to go now, Zara. It's my time. They want me to leave now. My mother is here with me and I want to go. I'm ready. This life is for the living. I've overstayed my visit.'

'I feel as if I'm losing you all over again,' Zara cried, her pale face bruised and blotchy from Jon's punch and her tears.

'I'll always be around you ... just not in you.' Maddy chuckled.

'But—'

'No buts, Zara. I must go. Love my daughter for me.'

Zara heard Maddy's voice soften as she began to fade. 'Bye, my darling Maddy,' she whispered back. 'I will never forget your strength, and the power of your love.'

'Love is the answer, Zara. Without that, there is no point.'

Zara nodded, and Maddy's pale shape rose up into the sky. Soft clouds appeared to stretch and feather behind her, wrapping themselves around her like two wings, lifting her out of sight. Then the sky was cloudless and empty.

The first things Pippa saw when she awoke were Zara's loving eyes and reassuring smile.

'Hush. We're safe now,' Zara told her.

For Pippa, held in her sister's arms, the last hour had been confusing and strange. Tilting her face, she looked up into the sky as if the answers resided there. Pippa hadn't physically seen Maddy on the boat, or seen her leave, but through her unconscious dreams, she'd heard her comforting voice, listened to her loving mantras, felt her breath and soft kiss on her skin. She turned to Zara for some sort of confirmation. 'Was Maddy here?' she asked.

Squeezing Pippa tightly, Zara could only nod, her heart breaking for her. 'And my father?' she asked, her voice sounding thin and strained.

Zara shook her head slowly. 'I'm sorry, Pippa, but the boom broke free in the squall and hit him in the head, knocking him overboard.'

Pippa said nothing for a moment, her heart beating with the confused emotions of a child, filled with a mixture of pain and relief. 'Is he dead?' she asked, her words faint and uncertain.

Zara paused. 'I think so.'

Pippa began to cry, tears slipping down her already salty face as troubled images tumbled through her mind. Unsure, muddled, Pippa – like Maddy before her – tried to make sense of her conflicting emotions. Why had her father, her golden protector, crossed that line? Why had he tried to do those things to her? She remained there, with her own grief and raw emotions, her unanswered questions, listening to Mathew's snores from under the cockpit table. After a while, she pulled away. 'Will Mathew be all right?' she asked

'He'll be fine.'

'Zara!' a distant but familiar voice called out.

'Izzy?' yelled Zara in genuine relief, twisting to see where the voice had come from.

Pippa extracted her body from Zara's. 'There!' she cried, pointing at a figure in the water, battling with the upturned *Phoenix* dinghy, trying to grasp onto the bent stern ladder.

'Izzy!' Zara cried again as she scrabbled to untie the tender cords in an attempt to give her easier access. 'I forgot all about you in the squall and the drama on board. Are you ok? How did you survive the sea?' she asked. 'I'm so sorry!'

Izzy looked up at two pinched and worried faces. 'It's ok, Zara, leave the dinghy, the rope's caught around the swim ladder anyway.'

Zara and Pippa moved back, allowing Izzy room to swing her lithe body over and around the obstacles. 'Anyway, I'm sure you had enough to handle here,' she added. 'I watched the squall from the beach and decided to stay there. I swam back once it was all over. Where's Mathew?' she asked, dragging herself up onto the deck, and sitting for a moment to regain her breath. Then, noticing Zara's swollen face and Pippa's injury, she added, 'You're both hurt!'

'We're fine,' Zara reassured Izzy, 'but there's been a casualty.'

'Mathew?' Izzy asked, looking around her.

'No, he's safe. He's over there.' Zara gestured to the lifeless form under the cockpit table. 'Slept right through the drama.'

'Slept?' Izzy questioned in disbelief. 'In that squall?'

'Yes. Jon put something in his drink. He went out like a light. I've checked on him and he's snoring, so I assume he'll come round when it wears off.'

'Where's Jon?' Izzy asked, aware of Pippa's and Zara's shivering as they glanced at one another.

'The canvas awning got loose, Jon got tangled in it, then the main boom broke in the squall, hitting him in the head and knocking him overboard.'

Pippa burrowed her body into Zara's.

Izzy walked around the boat, leaning over the sides and checking below. There was no sign of a body or the awning. Acknowledging the mess of the boat and the injuries on both girls, she knew there was more to this accident, but for now she needed to be practical. Zara and Pippa were wet, cold and in shock. She knelt down at Zara's feet and smiled reassuringly at Pippa. 'Do you know where Maddy kept her T-shirts and towels?' she asked.

Pippa pulled away from Zara and glanced hesitantly towards her before nodding.

'Perhaps you could go below and get some; and a large towel for Mathew too.'

Pippa nodded, gingerly approaching the cabin steps.

'Have you called for help?' Izzy asked, looking up at the loose boom.

'No. But the radio keeps shouting something about a Mayday.'

'Ok, let me try. Someone may have seen the squall and reported it. Looked pretty spectacular from out there. God! You were both so lucky,' said Izzy, looking around her.

'Not *God*, Izzy,' clarified Zara, whispering. 'I had Maddy helping me. It's so difficult to comprehend and impossible to explain.'

Izzy moved towards Zara. 'Try?' she said, placing a hand on hers.

Zara gasped for air, exhaling deeply before continuing. 'Maddy finally came out of me.'

'Thank God,' responded Izzy with relief.

'It was Maddy who created the squall ... to protect us from Jon,' Zara started to explain, her body shaking with delayed shock. Izzy held her hand tightly, squeezing it with encouragement. 'And when we were safe,' Zara paused, hiccupping with a sob, 'she left.'

Izzy grabbed Zara to her, hugging her tightly. Zara found a lump rise in her throat and she let out a pained sob. 'It was so awful, Izzy. I've never been so terrified.'

'Shush ... it's ok now,' whispered Izzy. 'You can tell me later, if you want to. Does Pippa understand what happened?'

Zara shook her head. 'Not really ... *neither* of us understands; things happened on deck that she didn't see, and I don't know what took place down below with Jon.'

Izzy remained quiet, her mind alive with unanswered questions.

'Where do you think Jon's body is now?' asked Zara, biting her lower lip in distress.

Izzy paused. She knew the strength of those currents, having swum against them on many occasions. 'He could be a long way from the boat by now. The currents could have towed him any direction.'

'Would he float?' asked Zara, shuddering at the thought. She had visions of old movies in which corpses sewn into canvas shrouds slipped overboard.

'I don't think so,' replied Izzy, not if he was caught up in the awning. Wet canvas is very heavy. Search and rescue will try to find him; you'll need to explain what happened and where he went down.'

'That should be interesting,' replied Zara, shivering at the prospect.

'Perhaps an abridged version, Zara – the truth ... without the Maddy bits,' suggested Izzy.

'And do I tell them about Jon's history and his real intentions towards Pippa?' Zara asked, her eyes boring into Izzy's.

'That's something you need to decide,' said Izzy.

Zara looked away. 'I can't,' she whispered, shaking her head. 'I hate the deceit, but the truth complicates everything, Izzy. And it's potentially damaging for Pippa too. Whatever transpired in the cabin earlier with Jon was enough to shatter her trust in her father.' Zara pushed back a wet curl from her face. 'She'll need time to process this and all her emotional strength to cope with the next few months ahead. Nathan's alerted the police in the UK about Jon, and by now my mother will have heard all about his past. All hell is about to break loose, especially when we turn up without him.'

'If I was your mother I'd want to kill him,' said Izzy.

'Looks like Maddy's beaten her to it,' Zara replied.

Izzy looked at Zara's troubled face. 'When you're ready, I'd like to hear what really happened here. I'm sure Mathew would too.'

Zara shook her head. 'You won't believe me ... but then again, you probably will.'

The voice on the radio came from the *Water Hawk*. Izzy rushed for the handset. Lifting and pressing the Receive button, she sank to her knees. 'Hello, *Water Hawk*,' she answered. 'We are anchored securely but have no main boom, no captain and no sailor aboard. One man down and one man overboard. We need assistance urgently,' she shouted into the phone, both hands tightly grasping the receiver, shaking with relief.

For so long, Izzy had held her emotions in check, for both Zara's and Pippa's sakes, but with the realisation that help was close at hand, she began to cry. The nightmare of the last few months was finally over. She'd done as Maddy would have wanted. As a result, Pippa was safe and Jon no longer a threat. Now she could concentrate on herself, beginning with healing the huge void that Maddy's death had left in her life.

Arousing Izzy from her thoughts, Pippa emerged from the galley wearing an old T-shirt of Maddy's that draped down both arms and past her knees like a dress. 'They're Maddy's favourites,' she explained, passing out towels and soft, dry clothing. Izzy held a T-shirt to her nose and inhaled. 'It still smells of her.' A faint smile playing on her lips. 'Thank you, Pippa,' she said, pulling the pale grey T-shirt over her slim, damp body. 'Much better.'

'Help's on the way, sweetie,' Zara told Pippa, smiling with

relief as she too pulled on one of Maddy's T-shirts. 'We've heard from the *Water Hawk*. Gareth's on the boat with them. They'll take us on board and someone else will bring the *Phoenix* home. We can get off this boat.'

'Will they find my father?' asked Pippa, a look of panic shooting across her face.

Zara knelt in front of her, taking her face in her hands. 'Someone else will look for him darling ... but not us.'

'Do I have to tell them ... anything about ...?' Pippa's bottom lip quivered as she touched her bruised forehead.

'No, darling, you don't have to tell anybody anything. I'll just say you hit your head when the boat got caught in the squall.'

Pippa nodded. Zara looked at her little face – so much for a child to absorb and process; her heart bled with pity.

Izzy watched and listened. Then, looking down at Mathew crumpled under the table, she winced. 'Shouldn't we try and make him more comfortable?' she suggested.

'I tried,' said Zara. 'I couldn't move him ...'

Izzy just nodded, acknowledging the hopelessness of the situation. 'So how do we explain his role?' she asked.

'He didn't have one,' replied Zara. 'He was knocked out, cold.'

Izzy recognised her twist on the truth and agreed that the simpler version from Zara would work, as neither she, nor Pippa, nor Mathew had seen Jon up on deck, or witnessed his fall overboard. Jon's accident was just that: a boating accident.

As all three faces peered under the table, a pair of the brightest blue eyes opened, right on cue.

'Well, at least we have a sailor on board now,' Izzy said, grinning.

Chapter 33

The Spanish newspapers carried the story of a freak twister hitting a sailing boat off the Balearic Islands, referring to it as a 'killer squall' with one loss of life and numerous injuries. Photos of the twister funnelling itself around the *Phoenix* were posted on twitter and Facebook. To the world, it was an unusual happening, a chance weather anomaly; to Zara, it was nothing short of divine retribution.

Jon's body was never found, despite the fact he'd dropped down beside the anchored *Phoenix*. Search teams trawled the ocean for days, following the currents and tides, but found nothing. Lisa was warned that her husband's body could turn up on one of the surrounding beaches, but having spoken to Nathan and learnt all she had, she didn't care if he never surfaced again.

After the necessary enquiries with the authorities in Majorca, Jon's accident was recorded as a drowning and his body registered as 'lost at sea'. Michael organised the necessary 'death in absentia' applications. He'd never liked Jon, but as always, he made sure the family were looked after.

'Befitting ending,' had been Nathan's remark when he heard Zara's edited version of events. She had made no mention of ghostly interventions; some things were best left unsaid.

⌒

While the formalities surrounding Jon's death were carried out in Majorca, Nathan wrote to Detective Martin Nesbitt back in the UK, passing over as much detail as he could remember of that night in Soho. He made reference to notebooks he had secured in his safe in Cuckfield, containing car registration numbers, descriptions of individuals and names and dates that may have been of use to the police in their investigations. He knew his time was short and he needed to ensure the truth was relayed as best as he could recall it. He would not stand trial and Jon would never be accountable now. Only Jimmy's side of the story remained.

Nathan carefully folded his last letter, placed it in an envelope and sealed it, sighing with relief. The timing was right now for him to put his final plan into action. On the mantelpiece in his room stood three envelopes, all containing carefully scripted letters: one for Martin Nesbitt at the Met, together with a key to his Cuckfield property and codes for his private safe, one for Zara and one for Lisa. Laying a hand on the note for Lisa, he bowed his head. 'Time heals, Lisa,' he said. 'And I hope in time you'll forgive me.' Checking again that the room was tidy, his things carefully packed into his bag beside the bedroom door, he set off towards the beach, his thin summer jacket over his arm. Tonight the pathway to the beach held no fears and he had no concerns regarding the steepness of the return trip; he'd no intention of making it back up.

Nathan removed the syringe from his jacket pocket, spread his jacket out onto the now cool sand and sat, finally making his peace with his God. Taking the morphine in his shaking hands, he began to quietly cry. Not for himself, but for everyone his life had ever affected, good and bad. There had been some very good – like the free clinics he financed in outer London, and the donations he gave to numerous charities and organisations, churches and children's hospitals. But despite his philanthropic gestures, Nathan's guilt continued to eat away at him, his body exhausted, the cancer now consuming any remaining life.

The letters in his room were apologies for what he'd done and what he now intended to do. He'd left enough funds for his body to be cremated in Majorca and his ashes tossed somewhere out in the ocean. He gave instructions that any remaining wealth and his home in Cuckfield should be given to Lisa; he'd always thought Jon's treatment of her financially brutish.

As the liquid entered Nathan's system he saw her, standing against the backdrop of the late-evening sky: her flaming red hair bright against the soft glow of the dying crimson sky, her green eyes sparkling back at him with compassion. 'Please forgive me,' he begged, one hand stretching towards the image as he felt his body lifting.

She smiled at him, her arms widening in welcome.

'I was so wrong,' he told her, as their arms met and the two of them looked down on his still warm body from up high.

'Come,' she told him, taking his hand.

They found him the following morning, lying on the sand, wrapped in his jacket, an empty syringe beside him, a trace of a smile on his lips. Nathan had found his forgiveness and, with that, his own peace.

Chapter 34

Nathan's confession, together with the directions to the riverbank in Staines, led to the discovery of eleven small skeletons. According to the coroner, some of the bodies had been in the water for many years. Nathan had confessed to his involvement in the accidental death of Rachael and the concealing of her dead body, but made no mention of any other victims. Jimmy supported Nathan's account and named Jon as the mastermind in the original case of the missing Rachael. He claimed to have no knowledge of any of the other remains.

Martin explained that although the DNA was of little use due to the length of time the bodies had spent in the water, dental records of the remains matched a number of children, all missing girls. When Martin's team searched the Wimbledon property, they found the hidden cache of victim spoils, all of which helped with identification.

Most of the children had been photographed prior to their deaths and their images sunk deep within the web to a site linked to a paedophile ring. Jimmy admitted that he had been responsible for taking many of the photographs, but knew nothing about any deaths. With Jon missing and Jimmy in custody, the ring began to falter, closing ranks and giving up a number of smaller links. Martin knew it would take years to break it down fully, but he'd started the dismantling. No guilty party would be safe, wherever and whatever their professional standing in society. That he promised.

Of the skeletal remains that were found, one was confirmed

as being Rachael O'Leary's. The discovery of this small body made Martin weep with relief; he'd searched for her for so many years. As promised, he made arrangements personally for a Catholic burial in a local church. That way, he could visit her, her own family being long gone. With Rachael finally laid to rest, he could sleep in peace for the first time in decades.

Lisa handled Jon's loss with composed dignity in public, mixed emotions in private. It seemed her short period with him had been built on deceit and pain – hers and others'. Pippa remembered nothing of that day on the water, or so she claimed, consciously burying the full details of the altercation with her father on the boat, her young mind refusing to process the full implications. And assured by Zara that nothing had taken place on the boat between Jon and Pippa, Lisa left well alone.

Although Nathan's gift of money and a home provided her with an alternative address, Lisa elected to remain in Majorca, preferring to stay out in the Pink Villa with Pippa rather than go back to Wimbledon and all its dark secrets. Over the years, Lisa came to forgive Nathan, seeing him as the troubled friend he always was. She would often walk down the beach to where he took his last breath, and talk to the ocean.

Zara and Gareth agreed to take over the house in Wimbledon, renting at a nominal amount via Michael for Pippa's future, their proviso being that Jon's study area be totally torn apart and absorbed back into the main house.

With Michael's help, Pippa was enrolled in an English school in Palma. Her time in the Pink Villa reinforced her love of the sea and boats, and she never thought negatively about the deaths of either Maddy or Nathan, believing they were still around the property, looking after her. Lisa too felt a sense of tranquillity around the place that had never been there before.

Shortly after Zara and Gareth's wedding in Majorca, Zara gave birth to twins; a boy and a girl, Jason and Hattie. As they grew, the age gap between Pippa and the twins seemed to lessen, the cousins growing closer. The Pink Villa became a place filled with joy, love and happiness, with Lisa in her element, as both mother and grandmother – just as Maddy would have wanted.

Izzy continued to paint in her studio shop in Ibiza's Old Town. Mathew made a number of visits there, as a friend, until one night, hugging her close, he kissed her goodnight in a way neither expected. From that day onwards, they found something within each other and became inseparable, sailing, painting and working daily together. Zara always wished that one day they would marry, but when asked, Mathew would only smile and flash his unbelievable blues eyes in Izzy's direction and she'd just laugh, their absolute pure joy infectious.

For Zara, out of all the pain and loss, good things had happened. It all just took time and a lot of forgiveness.

Epilogue

One word frees us of all the weight and pain of life;
that word is *love.*

Sophocles

They'd come to wish Pippa well: her mother, Lisa, Zara, Gareth and her two cousins, Jason and Hattie, and the ever-growing gathering of well-wishers. Pippa had always claimed that one day she'd sail around the world single-handed, and today, on her twenty-first birthday, they waited to see her off on her dream.

Despite her petite frame, Pippa stood with complete confidence, dressed in a pair of oversized orange waterproofs. Her short, blonde, sun-streaked hair blew softly around her face as she waved from her boat, the *Seraphim*, to the supporters and press.

The voice of a local reporter cut through the general buzz of commotion. 'Aren't you afraid of being lonely out there, on your own all that time?' he asked.

Pippa paused for a brief moment, smiling to herself. 'No,' she replied shaking her head. 'I'm never lonely.'

That night, as the *Seraphim*'s bow cut through the crystal waters, Pippa looked out at the endless grey sea surrounding her and felt a sense of peace and contentment. She'd inherited her love of the sea from her mother, Maddy, her courage from those whispered tales of 'avenging angels' and her rescue in Majorca. She'd crossed many wild seas since then, battling against storms, her faith in the powers of her constant protectors unchallenged. Looking up at the stars above her, Pippa called out to them: 'Ahoy there! We have a long trip ahead of us … are you joining me?' The gentle wind murmured back through the billowing sails, the waves breaking on the prow. Pippa smiled as she acknowledged the two small lights that suddenly appeared, dancing ahead of the cutting bow, lighting up the waters below.

'Welcome aboard, ladies! Prepare for starboard tack.'

Acknowledgements

There have been so many people that I need to thank for their encouragement and involvement with *Within the Silence*: to Imogen A. K. for the biological DNA advice, Peter W. for trust legalities, Nick P. and Charles A. for all things nautical. Any errors are entirely of my making. To my friends and family for their constant support and my long-suffering partner Charlie, who put up with my nocturnal scribblings and stepped outside of his factual comfort zone to re-examine the boating scenarios and fictitious Majorcan sea/landscapes.

A huge thank you to my publishing team at whitefox, my wonderfully diligent team of talented people that have once again helped bring my writings to print: the ever calm and patient George Edgeller, Berni Stevens, Jill Sawyer, DeAndra Lupu, and the very fabulous Anne Newman, my tireless editor who ensured each piece of jigsaw fitted correctly within the plot. My warm thanks also go to Fiona Marsh and Alice Geary at Midas Public Relations for their wise, considered guidance. Couldn't have done it without you all.

To each and every one of you who have helped me along the way with *Within the Silence*, thank you.

About the Author

With an artist and writer for a father and ballet dancer for a mother, Nicola was destined to go back to her creative roots. Having spent a decade in Australia, she returned to her birthplace, Surrey, to raise her family. Fascinated with the concept that she had lived before, Nicola studied and qualified as a hypnotherapist and past life therapist, using her personal insight and experiences to create the controversial plots for her thrillers. *Within the Silence* is her second novel.

Also by Nicola Avery

Whispered Memories

Nicola's compelling debut novel.

For the last three years, sleep has become an increasing source of terror for Emma Hart, with nightmares that have turned into chilling visions. Her newly married ex-husband, Joshua, wants custody of their three-year-old daughter, Amelia, and will seemingly stop at nothing to get it. What is it that Joshua hides? What shapes his behaviour, turning a loving husband into a cruel opponent?

Emma knows she needs to unlock her unconscious quickly, before the visions take over and she loses both her daughter and her mind. But how does she do that, and when the truth finally surfaces, for both of them, will they be prepared for what they might find?

A multi-dimensional love story, *Whispered Memories* is at once heartbreakingly sad, tender and warm. It is a debut that is as memorable as it is thought provoking.

Paperback ISBN: 9781911195252

Ebook ISBN: 9781911195269